When All Else Fails

Chin Up Tits Out

Miranda Oh

Couronne Publishing
WINNIPEG, MANITOBA

Miranda Oh
www.ohmirandaoh.com

Publisher:
Couronne Publishing
info@couronnepublishing.com
www.couronnepublishing.com

Cover design by Vanessa Mendozi
Images used under license Shutterstock.com

When All Else Fails; Chin Up Tits Out- Miranda Oh.
1st edition
ISBN 978-1-988497-01-3

This book is dedicated to my village. You all constantly fueled my patience, love, and strength. Without the people of my village, the Chin Up Tits Out series would not have happened. It would just be a random, twisted nightmare in my head. Also, a special shout out to Mary Jane and Merlot.

The anticipation nearly killed me. After Riaan's permanent residency finally got accepted, it was a whirlwind. We had solidified a "move to Canada" date and there was so much to do. Riaan and I had been working on getting his residency for four years. When it finally came through, the excitement was amazing, but then panic eventually settled in. He was packing up his life—literally everything he ever knew, everyone he had even been friends with, his entire family—into a couple of small suitcases that were about to be thrown onto a plane and shipped to the opposite side of the world.

Every time we spoke, I could tell he was feeling stressed and it started to make me worry a little bit. I had been so consumed with getting him into Canada that I didn't stop and think about the potential chance that he didn't like it here. I didn't stop to think what if he doesn't love Canada as much as I do and what if our love for one another wasn't strong enough to keep him here? What if the winters scare him off?

All these stupid questions and doubts raced straight to my heart, which in turn led to an unexplainable rush of tears. You know, a typical girl meltdown, where we sob for no apparent reason.

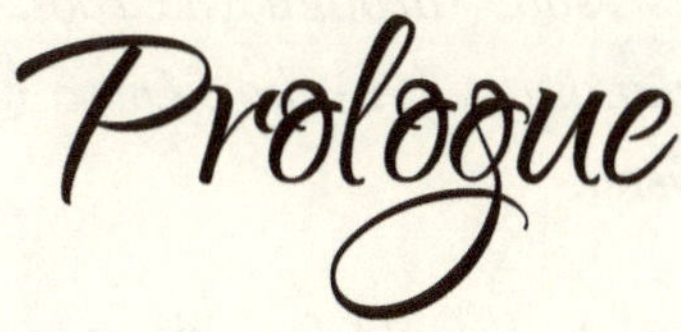

Prologue

As the car pulled up into my parent's driveway, a rush of excitement ran through my body. Everything from the tips of my toes to my cheeks lit up with butterflies.

You can do this Hadley! You've survived worse.

As I walk towards his white Ford Escape, I can see his eyes widen as I approach. He hopped out of his SUV and ran around the vehicle, eyeing me up and down as he pulled the gentleman card and opened the door to assist me in.

"Uh, wow. Hadley, you look amazing."
He stammered out.

My confidence level just shot through the roof. Yeah, he thinks I'm hot... damn it... I AM hot! Or so I kept trying to convince myself.

As I stepped into the truck, I could feel his eyes on my ass and I knew this dress was a winner. Thank goodness, I was finally starting to feel like one.

Bloody hell... I have the worst dry mouth. My mouth feels like I am chewing on a cotton ball... that stupid pipe. I should have brought gum.

As he gets into the truck, he checks me out from top to bottom admiringly while trying to process something intelligent to say. Nope, not going to happen. He sputtered out, "So, yeah, ready to stuff your face?"

I beg your pardon? Stuff my face? Did you really just ask me that?

I nervously look at my hands, which are carefully folded on my lap, "Uh yeah, I guess so. I haven't been to the Ivory Restaurant before and I love East Indian food. The flavours and spices are so exotic and rich."

After what felt like a very long drive, we finally arrived at the restaurant. Parking was atrocious, so continuing to be a gentleman; my date offers to let me out at the front door so he can find parking.

While waiting for him to park where does my head go?

Crazy Hadley's head goes to SHIT. Shit, shit, shit... I panic... He has dropped me off and left me here... I blew the date, I knew it. I can't do this.

I'm instantly sweaty, in all the wrong places, if you know what I mean.

Oh my god I had no idea my lady bits could sweat this much.

I ask the host for a table near the window and directly under a vent as I endeavor to get my sweat issue under control and so I have a clear view to see if he actually abandoned me, which will mean I am dining alone. The aromas from the food in this restaurant are heavenly and making my cotton mouth water, thank god, there is no way am I going to waste all the work it took to look as good as I think I do. I stare out the window trying not to gawk at every person that walks by, hoping it was my date. And there he is, so of course he didn't abandon me, as usual, it was just my crazy thoughts. Once he sat down, and settled in, he simply stared at me in silence.

Yes.... How may I help you?

After what felt like forever, I stuttered out, "So, how long have you lived in Canada?" Go figure, he was a black guy with an African name, so naturally I figured it would be a good conversation starter. At least I hoped it would be, as it was the best my brain could muster at that moment.

Before he could answer, our waiter arrived. "Is there anything I can get you two to drink before you hit the buffet for supper?" He politely asked.

"WINE!" I nervously spit out before even thinking. I tried to make eye contact with my date in agreement.

"Oh no, not for me. I don't drink while I eat. Just water for me please." He smiled at our waiter and crossed his hands neatly on the table.

You have got to be kidding me! I am sitting here with my arms tight against my body, my hands trembling under the table because my lady parts are still sweating and thanks to the cold vent above I'm trying to contain my high beams... and now I am drinking alone can this be any more humiliating?!

I try not to roll my eyes, but who is kidding whom here, and of course, he caught me. "Oh no, please Hadley, have a drink if you want. I am driving and want to save my drinking for the social later. Oh, did I even tell you about the social?"

"Social?" I quizzically asked.

I can't do a wedding social! Seriously! Too many people, too many happy people. Happy people getting married. What the hell am I doing, this date was supposed to be a positive step in my therapy not self torture! I can't do this, is it rude if I ask to leave now?

"Oh yeah, after supper I thought we could hit up a wedding social. It's a Filipino couple that my buddy knows. It should be a riot!" He smiled, quite proud that he came up with what he obviously considered an awesome master plan for a first date.

Little did he know I was dying inside with a big shit ass grin on my face as I faked appreciation. I was doing everything in my power to choke back a panic attack while waiting for my wine, so I could drink alone, on this first date, which I was not handling well at all.... Stupid therapist, PHD my ass!!! New definition for PHD; Pathetic Hadley Does it again... what does he know anyway.

"That sounds fun," I said with a shaky voice. My heart was screaming at me, telling me it was a bad idea. But my head is telling me to go. This is way out of my comfort zone, my therapist told me to go outside of my comfort zone, but this feels more like running naked across a football field just prior to kick off at the Super Bowl.

Everything about this was out of my comfort zone.

We dined and chatted throughout supper. By the time we were done, my nerves had calmed a bit, thanks to the wine. I was finally able to breathe without my chest feeling as if it was closing in on me. My hands were only clammy, not trembling and dripping with sweat anymore and the high beams had finally gone back down to where they belong. I felt like I was on a roll, then the bill came.

Do I reach for it? Do I ignore it? God, I haven't done this in so long. Do I offer to pay my share, or do I let him pay? What if he expects something in return?

"Ah, thank you sir." My date says grabbing the bill before I could even compile my thoughts.

How can something as simple as paying a dinner tab cause so much stress, and the night isn't even close to being over... Oh bloody hell Hadley, keep it together.

"You ready to go Hadley? I planned to stop at my buddy's place for a couple of drinks before the social, you cool with that?" He smiled with a twinkle in his eye, he was so proud of "the plan".

No, I want to go home is what I want to say, but a miniature form of my therapist appears on my shoulder again coaching me to go beyond my comfort zone... Stupid doctor, pain in my ass. Feels more like a devil on my shoulder and I am desperately praying for the angel to show up, but of course, I am not that lucky.

"Ah, yeah of course, that should be fun. Is it just the three of us going to the social?" I ask, trying to focus on breathing through this overpowering feeling of fear crawling up my legs like long arms from hell gripping deep into the pit of my stomach.

Breathe Hadley, just keep breathing.

"Oh, no I think there are eight of us going. You'll have to forgive my buddies. They are great, but all single, so you get to escort the seven of us." He chuckled to himself. Probably assuming I would like all the attention.

Seven guys... SEVEN GUYS and me... Hadley! What are you doing? Where is your brain right now, you are probably walking into some gangbang porno snuff video, or like my baba calls it...Punugraphy. This is all in your head girl, shake it off. Chin Up Tits Out. You can handle anything after the hell you have already survived. You got this... yeah I do... I can own these guys and the night. What did I just talk myself into?

"Oh I am one lucky girl, aren't I?" I chuckled out sarcastically, gently throwing a soft punch to his shoulder. "How are you ever going to compete with the other six for my attention?"

Too cocky? Ah, hell. This flirting shit is hard.

My date looked down pretending to watch his toe kick a pebble on the ground as he shook his head and blushed.

WAIT a minute... did I just make a black man blush? Hah – Hell ya Hadley!

"I am just kidding!" I quickly stammered out as soon as I realized I might have embarrassed him.

"I arrive with you; I leave with you. That's the golden rule." I chuckled out nervously.

What golden rule Hadley? You fool, you just made up some lame ass rule, all while boosting his ego and assuring him you will leave with him. What if he turns all creepster... Did I just sign myself up for a booty call? Is that even a booty call? Oh my God.

We arrived at his buddy's apartment and as we walked down the hall, you could hear a party brewing at the other end of the building. My date opened the door for me and as I walked in, I see six large black guys sitting back, legs spread eagle, beers in hand and chatting, sorry no, yelling amongst themselves. Did I just walk into some angry confrontation?

Is it an African thing? Do all Africans talk that loud? It sounds like a loud, angry conversation and yet, they are all laughing.
Breathe, smile and say hi.

My date proactively grabbed both of us a beer and guided me to the only open seat in the apartment. As I sit down, all six guys go silent and stare at me like I am a lamb up for slaughter. Then they all quickly stood up, graciously shook my hand and individually introduced themselves.

Stupid Hadley, there you go again letting your own anxiety and fear take over normal brain function...no I don't remember ANY of their names, let alone how to pronounce them. I was of course too shit scared to have anything actually register in my brain. How rude of me, I definitely have some practicing to do, is brain loss yet another symptom I should be discussing with my therapist...

After downing a couple of beers, I felt like I was calming down and could start to breathe again. No one was sensing my anxiety, so I was managing to hide it quite well. My hands were so sweaty that I had to wrap my scarf around my beer bottle, just so I could sip it without the bottle slipping right through them. But the point here is that no one noticed and we all seemed to be enjoying the evening.

Maybe it's my charming, intellectual self-shining through. Hell no, who is kidding who here, guys become oblivious when a pair of boobs walk into a room... DUH!

It was time to hit the social. Hadley is about to show up to a Filipino social with seven boisterous men from Africa. A little old white girl rocking up with her posse of black boys. Yeah, that's right! You can't see the irony in this yet, but believe me it's crazy in so many ways.

African time is an actual thing I was told. It's where you add at least two hours to any scheduled time. We showed up to this social so late that there was absolutely no parking anywhere close to the entrance whatsoever. I saw a temporary bus stop and sarcastically suggested we move it and park where the bus stop used to be.

They actually moved it and parked there. WOW, Brilliant I tell ya, simply brilliant.

As the group of us sauntered through the doors, looking like we owned the place, the fear started to creep up into the pit of my stomach again. My hands and feet started to sweat. My body was trembling and I froze instantly. I could feel my toes smoosh at the tip of my shoes. And yet again, sweat in all the wrong places as I felt a bead of sweat drop from the bottom of my butt cheek and run down my leg.

Oh my God, I can't believe I don't smell like a linebacker late in the third quarter. I hope no one saw that. Breathe Hadley, just keep breathing!

Everyone fanned out and went in their own direction. As my date started to walk into the social, my feet were still frozen in place. Look at all of these people, there were hundreds of them. I couldn't move my feet; I was stuck as if frozen in time. My date turned around and saw me standing there looking white as a sheet and feeling like a lost puppy.

"You okay?" He asked with concern, as he walked back to me.

"Yeah, yeah. It has just been a while since I've been to one of these. Just taking it all in." I smiled graciously while lying through my teeth.

The last wedding type function I was at, was my own. My heart was slowly crumbling into a million pieces. The pain was so real and intense, my eyes glazed over as I tried to get the pictures of my wedding out of my head. That is all in the past now. Keep breathing Hadley, chin up, tits out you can do this... no I can't, I want to roll into a ball to protect myself and cry because it hurts too much to be here.

He grabbed my hand, which broke the fog in my head and walked me through the crowd, dodging dancing people and children running everywhere. He got me a drink and suggested we dance. We danced and drank and eventually, my fear dissipated. After a few drinks and a few dances, the smile on my face actually became real. Was I really having fun? I had completely forgotten what it felt like to have fun and simply live in the moment.

It was totally the alcohol. But, if it meant I didn't have to feel pain and I could find drunken laughter, what the hell. I wasn't about to stop now.

The end of the night came around and as it turned out, I thoroughly enjoyed myself! I didn't want it to end though. I knew the ride home was right around the corner and I couldn't turn my mind off. If I go home, all the fear and pain will once again creep back to become my reality; I won't sleep; I will picture my life the way it used to be, when my life was the way I wanted it to be.

Partying with seven black guys was never something that I could have pictured as being part of my reality. But I was proud of myself for having made seven new friends and feeling happier in that moment than I had in months. I didn't want this feeling to end. I shimmied my shoulders and wiggled my butt into my date. I spun around trying to dance to the tune in the background.

Truth is I am SO tone deaf.... I have no idea if I am even keeping the beat... Hell, I know I'm not but this feels great! I totally and utterly dance like the stereotypical white girl; I am sorry for inducing that stereotype.

"So, I am not ready for this night to end yet. Want to head back to your place?" I whispered in my date's ear. The fear was creeping in again, it took every strength I had to fake confidence and sensuality.

His head sprung back from my face, he looked at me in surprise. "Yeah, of course! If that is what you want, let's go right now. Like right now" He grabbed my hands and dragged me towards the door.

Adios, motha fuckas...

CHAPTER ONE

My Happy Little Family

I lived on my own in a condo, which was located right downtown, for quite some time before Riaan was scheduled to move up to Canada. It was on the river, with beautiful walkways, parks, and cycle paths. The street was lined with a couple other beautiful condo buildings, unique boutique stores, restaurants, and markets. This was a dream come true for me as I worked so hard and saved almost every penny from the time I was sixteen to get here. I truly enjoyed living alone and having the entire space to myself. It was a completely feminine space. The condo had a deep purple themed design with flowers everywhere and oversized fluffy throw pillows that you could sink into while enjoying a glass of wine or champagne after a really long day at work. And yes, I did this often! The only thing was that Riaan would hate it as much as I loved it. I had a lot of work to do to get my home feeling as comfortable and as perfect as I could before he arrived. I removed anything girly and replaced it with African themed art and added a new paint job that gave it a masculine feel while still keeping a warm and inviting theme that I was quite proud of.

I had to do everything possible to make him feel at home, to make this feel like it was his as much as mine. So yes, I resorted to African artwork and masculine colors, don't judge me. It made sense in my head at the time and really made me feel quite grown up and mature.

By the time Riaan landed, I had turned my entire condo into a gender neutral, warm, and comfortable living space. A place where you walked in and felt a sense of tranquility and peace. I was so excited for

Riaan to see this when I brought him to his new home. I hoped he loved everything I did to make it feel like it was now his home.

Of course, my parents—Sam and Gwen—and my brother—Blake—all came over to celebrate with me prior to going to the airport to pick up Riaan. We each had a glass of champagne and together we toasted to perseverance and celebrated that love always prevails.

It felt like my prayers from all these years were finally being answered, all at the same time. I was overwhelmed with happiness, excitement, and of course horniness. It had been a very long time since we saw each other. Not to mention, for our entire first year of marriage, we were over 3,000 km apart. Every time I blinked, I saw my hot, hunky husband naked and standing at attention, literally and meta-phorically.

I blinked a lot that evening.

On my first trip to South Africa, I remember I was so excited and so nervous that I had an over-whelming feeling of jumping up and down, vomiting, and squealing with excitement all at the same time.

Well that feeling came back with a vengeance. I was excited, nervous, happy, and scared all in the same moment. I was an emotional basket case. I will never forget the expression on Riaan's face when he walked through the doors at the airport. His face lit up like a full moon on a clear night, his smile was so wide; if he didn't have ears, it would have wrapped around his head. That was a line his dear Ouma used and I loved it! My prince charming was finally, after years of fighting with immigration, HOME!

If it wasn't against the law, I would have run right through the airport customs glass doors and hopped on him right then and there. All I could think was; I'm going to get some. I'm going to get some. Nah, nah, nah, nah, nah, nah!

He strutted right up to the four of us standing there and we embraced in a massive group hug. I wanted him all to myself, but arms were flying everywhere and heads were bobbing back and forth, knocking into each other. At that moment, I couldn't help feeling so blessed, it was a post card moment... a happy family moment. Everything was perfect, everyone was here, my hubby was home, and I was the happiest girl in the world.

After we all parted our bear hug, Riaan asked, "So, is it time to celebrate yet?" while shaking my dad's hand.

"I got us some cocktails for the road, Riaan. We came prepared," my dad said as he fist pumped the air.

Riaan chuckled and swung his arm around me as we started to walk back to the car.

My life is perfect. Nothing in the world could wipe the joy from my face and at that moment, I was glad I had ears as well or my smile would have wrapped around my head.

It took us a couple of weeks to get all settled in. Riaan was getting acquainted to life in Canada and was slowly adapting to life with the McLearys. We are definitely a robust family that enjoys spending a lot of time together. He spent time getting to know a lot of my family and had the opportunity to meet most of my friends. I couldn't have asked for anything more. We were living like happily married newlyweds at last.

It wasn't long before Riaan started working for a local plumbing company and really settled in. He was really getting his groove on and was falling in love with the security that living in Canada had to offer. I finally had the financial security of our two incomes and no longer had to try squeezing water from a rock to stay on budget. That said, I still worked most weekends at festivals with my airbrush tattoo business to make extra cash. I can't explain the sense of peace I had every morning when I woke up. The first thing I'd see was Riaan's face on the pillow next to mine. Even nasty morning breath didn't deter us from early morning romps... we had a lot of time to make up for. The things that most couples considered mundane like cooking dinner was still so exciting to me. I got to prepare meals for someone who I loved and he appreciated my effort.

Summer came only a few months after Riaan's arrival to Winnipeg. I know most of the world cracks jokes about "Winterpeg" and mosquitoes large enough to carry away small children, but this is a ploy we Winnipegger's use to prevent the crazies from moving here. Truth is, the trees are so green and flowers are blossoming everywhere. Our sun doesn't set until 10 PM, so you get to enjoy the sweet smells of long, warm, summer nights. Our little part of downtown was so beautiful, I was so proud to share all the great things about our city with my husband. After work, we would stroll down by the river and find a bench to sit, light a doobie, people watch, and enjoy the scenery. So many happy people enjoying the great neighborhood we called home. We watched so many couples out walking their dogs, and as if we needed the inspiration, we eventually decided to get a dog of our own. We were going to become our own little family. We figured it would be a great prequel to having kids.

The universe was finally answering all my prayers. A gorgeous husband that loves me, a job as an event manager that I love, my airbrush tattoo business flourishing, a beautiful home, and now a DOG! Look at you Hadley, all grown up and shit!

Growing up, when my brother and I got a new dog, my parents were the main caregivers. My brother and I unfortunately were designated as the main Pooper Scoopers... we definitely got the shitty job!

Ha-ha, lame joke. But hilarious all at the same time... am I right?

We grew up with purebred boxers that were beautiful, strong, and had the quirkiest personalities. Dixie and Storm kept us all entertained and very safe. Storm was a male who would pee in the shoes of every guy that I had ever dated that was brave enough to come by and meet my dad. As much as I wanted a boxer in the worst way, to purchase one on our own was slightly beyond our budget. So, after searching online on Kijiji and in shelters, we finally put up an ad on Kijiji for ourselves; "Young couple looking for a four-legged fur baby". It wasn't long before we had a flood of emails from people asking to meet us. We found a beautiful blue Chinese Shar-Pei, his name was Keizer (yes, like the bun).

We immediately became a little family. Riaan was so proud and seeing him so happy and content was amazing. We would go for daily walks around the neighborhood then we would all eat supper together. We spoiled Keizer rotten; he even had a weekly bubble bath. Head and Shoulders shampoo works wonders for dogs. It made him smell so handsome and the bonus was it cut back on the dander and shedding. We would even go on adventures to Grandma and Grandpa's. My parents thought we were crazy, but I know they loved him as well.

We figured we should break Sam and Gwen in gently and get them used to being called Grandma and Grandpa with our dog before the real babies came. My parents loved it.

Keizer fit right into our family life; I was befuddled at the way everything turned out. I would catch myself smiling over nothing; it was as if all of my dreams had come true.

We had become one of those really sickening in love couples that makes goo goo eyes and is constantly hanging all over each other. We were "Barbie and Ken" just like my parents. If this is what they call the honeymoon phase of marriage, I was digging it and so was Riaan. Occasionally I was like WTF, stop being so sappy, but the truth was I was starting to embrace how cliché we had become.

We were living a life of sunshine and rainbows, but reality is you don't get rainbows without a storm... I was hoping we had more than enough storms in our past, but I had a strange feeling that we couldn't be that lucky.

Shortly after we brought Keizer home, our Canadian wedding date had arrived. Since my extended family and friends didn't have a chance to celebrate with Riaan and I back in South Africa, we wanted to have an opportunity to party and celebrate with them.

Let's be realistic here, who wouldn't jump on the opportunity to celebrate another day of happy marriage with their partner? I was lucky, I had three weddings to the same man and no divorce.

My mom and I worked tirelessly on my wedding dress for months. We had taken her wedding dress from back in the '80s, where lacy, poof, and more lace was in style. We removed the poof, adding some length since I am a good 4 inches taller than her, and took the time to meticulously add 2500 Swarovski Crystals throughout the dress. It was stunningly breathtaking; it also weighed about 50 pounds.

The morning of, everyone started to get ready at my parents' house. I had my four closest friends and family as my bridesmaids, they all looked stunning;

not to mention I found them their bridesmaid dresses for $80 after taxes.

Bride on a tight Ukrainian budget I tell ya!

The five of us were all dolled up and looking like we belonged on the front page of a bridal fashion magazine. I sat there in disbelief that everything had turned out like this. Sometimes while fighting through life, it is difficult to envision what the future may hold. We get so consumed with the here and now and the struggles in front of us that we forget to take a second and appreciate what we have. My world froze in that moment of time. I saw how my life had ended up, and I was blissfully happy, this day was going to be perfect.

We chose the Millennium Centre to hold our ceremony and reception; a historical old bank, with four storey vaulted ceilings, marble flooring, walls and pillars. Old antique furniture and accessories were strategically placed, offering inviting nooks to sit and simply enjoy the view. There were over 300 candles lit and turned on.

Yes, I got the battery-operated ones, less of a fire hazard I figured.

The tablecloths were black and white damask, with a dark purple rose runner lying across the middle. Our centerpieces were clear, glass vases that stood at a mere three feet, and were shaped like the Eiffel Tower. They were filled with tiny, glimmering, purple beads and topped with black ostrich feathers that mimicked palm trees. The theme was elegance with a hint of old Hollywood.

Riaan and I asked my godfather to perform the ceremony for us, and right after the ceremony the party started. It was a perfect day. The ambiance, the company, the party, the food, everything was absolutely perfect. Everyone at the wedding was up and dancing, not a single solitary soul was sitting. At one point, even the staff joined in the fun. By the end of the night, when Riaan and I were saying our Good-bye's to our beloved guests, we were both feeling super happy and a little tipsy. We gathered our things and moseyed on down the street to a hotel honeymoon suite we had booked for the night.

"Tonight is our night babe. Tonight is our night babe." Riaan sang while carrying the train of my dress and dancing down the street. People were honking and shouting celebrations from passing cars. I chuckled, threw my hands in the air, and danced to his tune alongside of him.

Both of us were tone deaf and drunk...what a sight for sore eyes.

We got to our hotel room, it was gigantic. There was way more than the two of us needed to sleep for 7 hours... ha-ha ...sleep. I excused myself for a moment to go to the bathroom, in hopes of getting the 20 something small buttons undone from the nape of my neck to my bum. I struggled for what seemed like an eternity. I got all hot and sweaty, and frustrated. My hair was getting into my face, my eyelashes were falling off, needless to say, the opposite of wedding night sexy. I gave up with about five buttons to go, I tripped and flew out of the bathroom, letting out a yelp.

"Babe, can you please help me up." I reached my hand out from the floor.

No movement or noise.

"Riaan!" I shouted a bit louder, struggling to try and get up to my elbows. Lace, dress and white poof was everywhere...
Remember 50 pounds of dress... everywhere.

He didn't move. I finally got my ass up and rolled myself over so I could crawl over to the bed. I playfully slapped the bottom of his foot. He was lying face first on the edge of the bed. No response from him.

"Hmmm... Hello? Are you awake?" I playfully tickled his toes.

Then I heard his snore. He only snored when he was really drunk and passed out.

"Well I guess I'm sleeping in my dress." I smiled to myself and passed out next him.

It wasn't pretty, nor romantic, but it was my life, and everything was great.

About a month had gone by since Keizer joined our family and I was giving him his weekly bath. With all his wrinkles, I had to dig deep and really massage everything, plus he liked it and kind of moaned. It made me giggle every time. As I was rubbing under his chin, I found a lump.

Hmm... It feels like a ping pong ball.

I rolled it around in my fingers, watching Keizer intently, seeing if he reacts in anyway. Nothing. That's odd.

"Riaan, babe, can you come here for a second?" I hollered.

He sauntered in nonchalantly.

"Can you feel this?" I said pointing to Keizer's neck.

"Feel what?" He said grabbing for my left boob, while giggling to himself.

I flinched away laughing and snorting in some of Keizer's shampoo bubbles. "No, ha-ha. Not that babe. Please check it out" I pointed again, to where his lump was.

"What is THAT?" his voice went all high pitched and cracked as he felt it.

"I am not sure; I guess we should go to the vet to find out." I said pushing a smile through my anxiety.

Keizer just became part of our family and now he is lumpy and probably going to die. Just great! Yes, lumps automatically mean death in my eyes. If I am freaking over what is most likely a huge bug bite on my dog, how am I ever going to handle children... Oh my God, I am pathetic, how do moms do this? Don't judge me.

We packed him up and took him down to the vet. This was all new to Riaan and me. We both grew up with dogs, but always had our parents there to take care of the serious stuff when it came to our pets. This time, we were on our own and we had to take care of the serious stuff.

Definitely sucks having to be a responsible adult caring for something or someone other than yourself.

Keizer didn't like going to the vet, it was like he knew shit was about to hit the fan. I literally dragged him in while Riaan pushed his ass from behind.

Definitely not a proud moment. Everyone else there seemed to have no trouble getting their pets to behave... Mortifying. We couldn't even control our dog and we were actually considering children.

The vet gave Keizer a full examination and played with him a bit. When it was time to give us the news, he asked us to "take a seat" in a stern but calm voice. The three of us, including Keizer, sat obediently.

Atta Boy, yay, he learned something. Such a good puppy!

"After a full examination of Keizer, it looks like he has Lymphoma, a type of cancer in the dog's Lymphatic system. We could do a biopsy on the tumor in his throat to be certain, but he has multiple lumps throughout his body."

"So, what are our options here Doc?" Riaan asked while ferociously petting Keizer.

Keizer was loving it.

"Well, we could do a number of things. If you leave him be, he might have three months of healthy, happy living. Or we could look into Chemo treatments, which would cost roughly $5,000 a month. Ultimately, it is your decision. I could provide different payment options for you as well in regards to the treatment. However, it still isn't guaranteed that he would survive through it all. Plus, the treatment would make him very sick, very quickly." He said with empathy in his eyes.

I know we have only had Keizer for a few weeks, but I loved him so much already. He was our first little baby. We had a happy little family here, and now I may have only three months left with him. The rug just got yanked out from under our happy little lives. Well this sucks...

"I'll give you guys a couple of minutes to discuss some options amongst yourselves. I'll see you in the waiting room when you are done," the vet said. As he got up and left, Riaan and I were cuddling Keizer who, by the way, was totally fine; not a care in the world and totally confused as to why his two owners were now blubbering idiots and paying so much attention to him.

"Babe, I think we should just spoil him and love him until he isn't happy or healthy anymore and then we can put him down with some dignity. It will turn out to be a good practice round for us," Riaan said as he grasped my shoulder and pulled me in for a hug.

Well that made me cry, obviously!

So, that is exactly what we did. On the way home, we stopped and bought him some really nice dog cookies and made sure he was loved and spoiled rotten. We let him up on the couch and in the bed at night. He farted so bad, it would literally stink us out of the room nightly. But, we vowed to do this and by darn, we were holding to our promise. We were striving to be amazing doggie parents and we were.

It was almost 90 days since our appointment with the vet when the infamous morning came. Keizer refused to get out of his kennel. After coaxing him out for what seemed like hours, as he tried to step out of his kennel, his back legs gave out and he peed all over the place. The poor dog was humiliated and I was devastated because I knew the time had come. I called Riaan at work sobbing, "Babeeeee, he is dying. He can't walk or stand, and he is peeing everywhere. What do I do?"

"Okay, give me an hour. Let me finish this job and I will come home to check on the both of you." He said in a calm voice.

Ah that voice, just warms me up. I can face anything with my husband at my side. Instant calm when Riaan does that.
Hubby to the rescue.

Of course, when Riaan walks into the condo, Keizer loses his shit and starts to bounce off the wall. So, the complete opposite from the half dead dog I have been dealing with for the last few hours.

"I SWEAR he wasn't like this 15 minutes ago. He couldn't even get up without his legs giving out on him, and he has peed on me twice, TWICE Riaan," I sobbed. I had cried on and off so many times that morning. Every time Keizer would move and he looked in pain, the tears would pour out of my eyes uncontrollably.

I turned into a blubbering idiot. Puffy eyes, snot-filled nose, and a pounding headache.

"The vet said this would happen, we need to make a decision Hadley." He said calmly and quietly. I refused to look at him.

"Had, babe. Look at me." He sternly said.

"UGH, I don't want to be an adult right now" I whined. We both knew we had to make the tough decision right away and both of us were avoiding saying it first.

So we called the vet together.

That Friday afternoon when everyone was getting ready for the weekend, we were packing up our dog to put him down.

Our lives had turned sad so quickly.

The procedure was simple and painless for the dog. Riaan and I were devastated; we must have sat in the room with Keizer afterwards blubbering for up to an hour. Thankfully, the staff at our vet's office were compassionate and patient with us.

We went home that night defeated and exhausted. As we walked into the condo, it reeked of dying dog, a mixture of dog hair, pee, drool, and the memory of Keizer. We looked at each other and shook our heads in agreement that we would just leave it for the night. We cracked a bottle of wine; poured the entire bottle into two glasses; and sat in bed and drank in silence with a couple of scented candles lit, you know, to mask the smell.

We both silently took the time to appreciate our chapter with Keizer, even if it was short. As much as it was completely out of our control, we both felt like we failed. The only positive I could take from this was that together we were so much stronger and I knew we could handle anything... or so I thought.

7:00 AM rolls around that Saturday morning. It was a nice, crisp, fall day in mid-November. As my alarm goes off, I roll out of bed and zombie walked to the coffee maker. Riaan and I had made a deal to 'de-dog' the condo that day—give the condo a full sweep from top to bottom—and have a fresh start. I wasn't even finished putting the water in the coffee maker when I heard Riaan gasp.

"Hadley, come here. NOW!" he yelled out from the bedroom.

I rushed to our room to see what was going on and I saw him sitting on the edge of the bed feeling his collarbone, shirtless and staring in the mirror.

"What is it?" I asked a little out of breath.

Yes, I was out of shape. I was in love shape, okay. Don't judge me on five steps making me out of breath. Shit happens, love happens. Hell, life happens.

"I have a lump." He said, still rubbing his collarbone, not taking his eyes off the mirror.

I knelt down on the ground in front of him. I gently removed his hands from his collarbone and there it was, staring both of us in the face. A lump. It looked identical to the one Keizer had in his neck, just not covered in dog hair.

This can't be happening right now. Shit damn hell, shit damn hell, keep it together Hadley! Your husband needs you to be calm, so be calm. But I knew my face was as white as a sheet and not looking calm at all. Shit damn hell.

I slowly composed myself and looked up from Riaan's shoulder to his face. We made eye contact for a split second and without a word being spoken, we got up, got dressed and headed to the nearest emergency room.

CHAPTER TWO

Lumpity Lump Lump Lump

You could only imagine the looks we got from the staff in the hospital. We spent the entire day in the downtown hospital emergency room. This is, of course, the hospital ER that closely resembles what you would see on a TV show. That day, we saw a large woman with a butcher knife stuck in her thigh and as she shuffled past us, we saw she had a steak knife or what appeared to be a steak knife hanging out of her shoulder blade. We watched a guy covered in blood and handcuffed to a gurney being pulled in from an ambulance and accompanied by at least half a dozen police officers. Needless to say, it was a not so typical day in your average emergency room and here we were; silently waiting. A crazy couple who thinks they have a lump that matches their dead dog's cancer lump seemed to be low on the staff's priority list.

When we finally got to see a doctor, they examined Riaan and their diagnosis was 'environmental'.

"We don't see anything out of the norm here for you Riaan. It is most likely due to it being your first fall season in Canada. Just monitor it and follow up with your family doctor," the doctor told us.

We felt like we were overly sensitive with this lump and that possibly, this doctor and their staff weren't taking us too seriously.

Honestly, how could they?

We booked an appointment with my family doctor for the following week. Dr. O we called her. She was this short, Polish woman with spiky, blonde hair and always wore high heels. She was spunky, fun, and very good at her job. She would always make sure she tested for everything and anything, she was extremely thorough. I figured if it was nothing, she would assure us that we were okay. We waited to see her for four or five hours on a Thursday evening. The sun was down and the entire office was closed. It was just the two of us and Dr. O left in the office by the time she got around to seeing us. The place was empty, even her office assistant had left for the day.

She walked into the examination room, looked Riaan up and down, pulled her glasses down her nose and turned towards me, "Is this your husband from South Africa? Is this the guy you have been talking about for years?"

"Yes ma'am, Riaan is finally here. But we have to get you to check something out for us. He has a lump on his collarbone. The doctors at the hospital said it was environmental, but we both think it is something different. We just put down our dog that had Lymphoma. I know this sounds super silly, but the lump showed up the day after we put down our dog." I said cautiously hoping I didn't sound as crazy as I knew I did.

"Well, that is odd, let me check it out. Shirt off Riaan." She pushed her glasses towards the bridge of her nose and started to rub her hands together to warm them up.

"I see..." she hummed as she was feeling Riaan's collarbone and neck.

"Hands up, over your head" she directed with a nod of her head. Then she took to groping his armpits and digging into them. I watched Riaan's face flinch when she dug in deep.

"Well, I don't think it is anything to be overly worried about, but I do think you should go to an oncologist."

Naïvely I asked, "What is an oncologist?"

She tilted her head down so her eyes looked up over her eyeglass frame at me. "Ah...a blood doctor. She is one of the best in the country. I will arrange for you to see her Saturday morning at 9 AM in the hospital emergency room. Don't be late."

"OK." I said, as I packed up our things to head home.

I had no idea what I was just told by this doctor, zero understanding. My stomach is doing back flips on me and feel like I am going to puke. All intelligence obviously escaped me as I knew what an oncologist was. My great baba had passed away a couple of years ago from cancer and her oncologist was the same doctor. we were going to see. But in this moment, I honestly remembered none of this. I was struck with panic and all I could think about was keeping it together for Riaan.

Thirty something hours later, we found ourselves walking into the emergency room eagerly awaiting what this 'blood doctor' has to tell us. Since the lump popped up, Riaan and I had become snippy to one another. The stress was eating away at our patience. We told no one that we were going to see this doctor as we didn't want to stress anyone out. Although, that left no outlet for release for either of us. So, naturally, the brunt of each other's anger and fear bounced between the two of us and slowly percolated to a boiling point.

We were escorted by a very pleasant nurse to a private room after we stated that Dr. Priscilla Morris was expecting us. Riaan was asked to get out of his street clothes and to put on the hospital gown they provided. Of course, Riaan had reached his boiling point and was angry, bitchy, irritable, and up until now, had directed it all at me. After the nurse left, he just threw the gown off the bed, took off his shirt, sat back, and crossed his arms.

"Babe, put on the hospital gown." I sympathized with him.

"NO! It is unnecessary; I am not a prisoner here. They are just checking out this fucking lump, I don't need a hospital gown. I am NOT sick." He snapped. In all the years that I had known Riaan, I had never seen this side of him. I was so afraid and felt completely helpless, as I knew it was his fear talking and not the caring man I married. I crossed my arms, sat back, and looked down at my lap. It wasn't worth the fight, so I sat praying silently.

I have always been more of a spiritual person than a religious one. I figured rules in life are simple... be a good person because it is the right thing to do. Do good things and good things will come to you; Karma is real. Nevertheless, in that moment I hoped that

God and every other power in the universe could hear my pleas.

After what felt like forever, Dr. Morris briskly walked into our room. She was a tiny sprite of a woman, standing maybe at 5 foot 5 inches. I am guessing that she was in her mid-fifties. She was certainly not what either of us expected, as if we even had a clue as to what to expect. Her hair was shaved almost right down to the scalp and was salt and pepper in color. She had high and standing at attention tattooed on eyebrows and big, juicy lips covered in dark pink lipstick that could have made me envious if the circumstances were different. In short, she was stunning and in a single word, confident.

"Hi, Dr. Morris." She said, pushing out her hand abruptly towards Riaan's to shake it. At this point, Riaan still had his arms crossed and was leaning back on the bed. He abruptly moved to meet his hand with hers and gave her hand a brisk shake.

"Let's have a look-see at what we have here. Where is your hospital gown?" she asked Riaan clearly knowing it was on the floor next to where she stood.

"Oh, I didn't put it on yet." Riaan looked immediately ashamed, trying to avoid eye contact with my annoyed eyes. He started to get up off the bed.

"That doesn't matter" she waved it away and pushed him back on the bed. The next thing I knew, she popped up on the bed and sat right beside my husband without saying a word.

"Let's get a good feel in and around your lumps here." She said while groping and digging into Riaan's neck, armpits and chest. "Hmm.... Yup. Ah, Yup! Okay, let's check this, yup!" she said talking to herself while manhandling his body.

My God woman, please tell me what you are doing? I felt nausea crawling up my throat and poor Riaan had no idea as to what was transpiring.

"Well, looks like you may have Hodgkin's Lymphoma, early stages. I will need you to go to the Grace Hospital to get a biopsy and then once you are done there, you will need to go to Health Sciences Centre to get a PET scan done. We will start chemo sometime in February. So, you should have a great Christmas this year." She said all while sounding as if she was discussing paint colors for a bedroom wall.

I didn't hear anything. Nothing she said registered. Did you just say my husband has cancer? A biopsy? What the hell is a PET scan? My ears were ringing, my stomach was flipping, and my body was trembling. I wasn't even the patient; I can't fathom how Riaan feels.

I tried to look across the room at Riaan but every-thing was blurry.

So much for being the strong wife. I can't fall apart when he needs me most.

"Will I die doctor?" Riaan softly asked looking down at his feet.

"Well of course you will! We are all dying. If you are asking, whether or not **this** cancer will kill you? No, probably not." She states casually, while washing her hands.

She walked over to Riaan, patted him on the shoulder and said, "don't worry, we will fight this. You are young and have that on your side." She then looked at me and winked.

What does that even mean? She winked; does that mean there is more that I need to know? Is there some secret that she cannot yet share?

She left the room as quickly as she came in, leaving Riaan and I sitting there in disbelief. We both stood silently staring off into the distance trying to process what was just said to us.

Hadley, your husband has cancer. Hadley, you are the wife of a cancer patient. How do I do this? How do I be a strong and loving wife when he is angry at the world and it feels like he is blaming me every time he even glances in my direction?

After a couple of minutes, I walked over to Riaan to give him a hug. He quickly turned and shrugged me off.

"Not now Hadley. Let's just go get this biopsy done, so I can go home." He moved me aside and left the room.

It was that exact moment where it felt like we were farther apart than when we lived on opposite sides of the world. How do I be what he needs most when he looks at me as if I was the cause of all his pain and anguish?

The 25-minute drive to the Grace hospital was silent, no talking and no radio. Every couple of minutes, I would glance over to look in Riaan's direction. He sat rigid and turned slightly to the passenger door as I was driving. His arms were crossed so tightly over his chest that his hands were white and his gaze was completely glossed over. His eyes were open but I knew he saw nothing but red anger and the blackest fear. The tension in the air was so thick that it was hard for both of us to breathe.

My heart was crushed. I was able to fight so fiercely for us and our love to get him to Canada but now I was helpless. I had no idea how to reach the man I loved more than life itself. I couldn't comfort someone who seemed to hate me. Logically I knew he didn't and that it was just the world attacking us yet again. Where was my chin up tits out strength? No matter how hard I tried I couldn't find it or fix anything in this moment?

I reached over to try to hold his hand. No success, he just moved it away. He didn't break his stare either.

I felt hopeless and more alone than I have ever felt in my entire life. I couldn't even begin to think how helpless he felt.

We got to the Grace Hospital. As we pulled in, I asked Riaan if he could give me a moment and that I would meet him inside.

Silence.

He opened the door and walked straight into the hospital without saying a word.

As soon as I saw the door close behind him and I knew he couldn't see me anymore, I broke down into tears. My chest was heavy, my head was pounding, my ears were ringing. I couldn't breathe, I couldn't see straight, I started to heave and hyperventilate. I completely unraveled in the car.

After a couple of minutes, I caught my breath and composed myself. I took a tissue and wiped my face off and reapplied my make-up. I found eye drops in the glove compartment and dropped a couple of drops into each eye. I picked up my phone, hands trembling, and called my parents.

"Good morning beautiful, how is your Saturday going?" my mom asked in her usual cheery mood.

"Riaan has cancer, Mom." I said. It was the first time I said it aloud. Immediately after saying it, I burst into tears again. When I think back, I believe what actually came out of my mouth was "Like husband, like dog, stupid fucking lump". This was one of those moments where I didn't need to be strong, I felt safe enough with my mom to show how truly angry I felt. I hoped she could make everything better like she always does. Even though I knew my mom couldn't pull a rabbit out of her proverbial hat this time, I naively hoped for just a moment that she could.

Mommy, please make it go away.

"Where are you guys now?" My mom's tone went into instant mom voice.

In between sobs, I managed to spit out, "The Grace".

"Your dad and I are on the way. Breathe honey, everything will be okay." She said as you could hear her banging around trying to get her things together.

"I have to go into the hospital. Riaan is in there right now and we have to see another doctor today." I cried out.

"See you soon." She said reassuringly.

Once that dreadful day had come to an end, we went home exhausted, cranky, dumbfounded, and completely numb.

Early in December, Riaan was no longer able to work because the cancer grew so rapidly. With Christmas closing in and only one income, the money I was able to save before Riaan arrived was quickly disappearing. I hadn't realized how much I hated cigarettes until then. It never bothered me before that my husband smoked and had smoked from the time he was sixteen until his cancer diagnosis. Cancer in your life changes things no one ever could have imagined. A pack of cigarettes was close to $20 and Riaan was smoking 4-5 packs a week with his added stress. This was quickly draining my savings and quickly draining my patience, so I took on a third job making gourmet donuts for a small boutique store because the hours were flexible and they paid in cash. I was determined to keep my independence, keep my husband happy, and give him everything he wanted.

It was almost Christmas and with it being Riaan's first ever white Christmas, we tried our best to stay positive and put on a happy face. We both agreed that telling his parents around this time of year would devastate them. He didn't want to cause any 'trouble' as Riaan called it; he was always worried about how his mother might react and we were already stressed enough. He insisted we keep it from them and only tell them if it was really necessary.

The weeks over Christmas and New Years were quiet. Riaan's tumors were growing every day, he grew physically weaker, and every couple of days he would have a new lump pop up somewhere. The lumps looked like golf balls just under the skin. They didn't hurt him to touch them or poke them.

Believe me, I tried. We both became quite obsessed with them. We even gave them names, which I know is weird as shit... but we discovered when cancer is in your life, all-sane thought goes out the window. We had Franken lump, Jerk Face, Larry the Lump, and Butter Ball.

The tumors were causing severe internal pain throughout his body and joints. I become completely useless to my husband and I felt like I was more of an annoyance than a comfort. We would go to bed, like newlyweds do, curled up in each other's arms, it wasn't long after a couple minutes we had to move away from each other because it was causing him too much pain. A few hours into his deep sleep, he would start to sweat and shake with pain, but he would stay unconscious. Nightly, I would be woken up by rolling into a sopping wet puddle of sweat. I'd turn on my bedside lamp to check on Riaan and he would be soaked through his clothes and sheets. His tremors would start at his head and it would move through his body like a wave until it hit his toes. This, we were told, was a common symptom. I wish someone had a handbook for spouses so I didn't feel so useless and so we could at least prepare in advance for what might happen.

Common symptom my ass!! Imagine a pee shiver that starts at your head and moves through your body all the way down to your toes.... but constantly back and forth, up and down... All. Night. Long. His body would vibrate. When it stopped, I would sometimes start to fear that he was dead. I had no idea what to think anymore. Watching someone you love in so much pain and not being able to do anything to help is the worst feeling in the world.

When it started, I would try and wake him up, but he would unconsciously lash out at me, roll over, and start to shake all over again. I would mention it in the morning to him and he would look me in the eye broken and apologetic because he had zero recollection of it happening. Eventually, it got so bad that he moved into our spare room so I could get enough sleep to go to work at two and sometimes three jobs the next day.

By the time New Year's rolled around, my savings were completely depleted from all the pain medication and other drugs that were not being covered by Medicare or insurance. Because Riaan wasn't a citizen yet, he wasn't eligible for unemployment insurance or any compensation. We were down to just my salary and the cash I could bring in when I could work doing airbrush tattoos and making donuts, but this became less and less as Riaan needed more and more care.

Great, just fucking great. Thank you, Visa. The medical bills were piling up far faster than I could pay them. But I refused to ask for help even though my parents constantly asked and offered. I just couldn't bear the feeling of having failed yet again. I failed my husband and he now has cancer. I was supposed to make a perfect life for us, but I couldn't even manage that.

I approached my manager at the catering company where I did all the event planning and explained to him my situation. He had to, unfortunately, decline my request for a raise to help support Riaan and myself. He explained that it just wasn't feasible and if he could, he would. I started to outsource other jobs, looking for anything and everything with a big enough pay cheque to keep the roof I worked so hard for over our heads, food in our stomachs, and pay for the medications and treatments Riaan so desperately needed to stay alive. It wasn't long before I found a call centre that promised me over double what I was currently making. Being blind-sided by cancer, having no money, and just being completely overwhelmed, I jumped on the opportunity. I up and quit my catering job and started working at this call centre, pumped and ready to provide.

Nothing can stop me. For a moment, I felt like my old self, like I could conquer the world... I found my Chin Up Tits Out strength again and our love will prevail. Everyone deserves a second chance, right?

A week into this new world turned into complete and utter hell for me. The job wasn't what was promised, neither was the pay cheque, and the hours left me so little time to be able to care for Riaan that I felt like I was going to die. So, by mid-January, not only was I a twenty something year old wife of a dying husband—who was brand new to the country and experiencing his first winter EVER—I was now also jobless.

How are we ever going to survive this? Truth is I didn't know the answer... Complete ugly breakdown. I turned into a puddle of monumental size from crying, not sleeping, working three jobs, and still not being able to save my husband's life. Thank you Dr.

Morris for telling me I have already gone above and beyond, even if I didn't really believe her. Now she had the pleasure of caring for my husband with cancer and me and my breakdown which just led to feelings of even more inadequacy.

My Brother Blake's 20th birthday was right around the corner, we were looking forward to something positive to celebrate. Both Riaan and I were not working, Riaan's health and morale had deteriorated drastically. His tumors were growing so rapidly that we had Rian rushed into the emergency room where we first met Dr. Morris, who was there waiting for him. She once again popped up onto the hospital bed next to Riaan.

"Well look at those little buggers." She said poking and prodding Riaan's upper body. He had lost some weight and was looking skinny and fragile, the skin on his back clung to his ribs. In fact, he had become nothing but skin, bones, and tumors, as there was no fat anywhere on his body... just lumpy painful tumors.

"Give me something that can help me Doc. This pain is not fun, eh?" Riaan said with a slight chuckle to hide his fear.

"Okay, I am going to put you on Prednisone, 100 mg a day, for 10 days. Once you are done the 10 days, we will start you on chemo shortly after that." She said abruptly, scratching all the info on a prescription sheet and tossing it to Riaan.

"Oh, I almost forgot to ask. Do you two plan on having kids one day?" She barked at us.

"That is the plan." I chimed in, with what I hoped was a smile on my face.

A little Riaan running around right now would be something that would make us smile again. It would give us both something to hope for, a possible future.

"Ok, you are both young so I assumed so. You will need to go to the fertility clinic, to freeze your sperm before you start treatment. I can call and get you in this afternoon. Are you free?" She said as she dialed a number into her old desk telephone.

Hmm, you tell me... my hubby is sick and can't work and well, me I went a little crazy as well so I don't have a job either. Of course we are free. Nothing better to do than hit a clinic where my husband has to wack spank the monkey... bang the bologna, spank the carrot, pull the goalie, choke the chicken... or whatever guys call it when they jerk off.

"Yes." We both said in unison.

She muttered quietly into the phone for a minute, put it down, and looked at us. "Okay, it is set up, go there right now."

"So, with this chemo, will I lose my hair Doc?" Riaan softly said.

"Oh, hell yeah", she said raising her hand in the air for a high five.

Seriously?

Riaan hesitated.

"Oh, for Christ's sake, children. I lost my hair and have been battling cancer for the last 7 years and look at me. I look awesome!" Dr. Morris said doing a happy dance on the spot.

Both Riaan and I chuckled, a sense of calm wafted through the air for a moment. Her confidence had a way of calming both of our fears.

Ahhhh, I can breathe for a minute now. If Doc Morris is that awesome, Riaan can be that awesome too... right? I mean tattooed on eyebrows aside; she was a pretty savvy broad. I liked her vibes.

We went straight to the fertility clinic after the meeting with Dr. Morris. I couldn't believe that my mid-twenty something year old husband and I need to go freeze his sperm. The task we were set out on was something I never pictured in our futures.

"I can't believe I have to jizz into a fucking cup!" Riaan angrily spat out as he stepped into the car.

"Well it is a precaution; the chemo will kill your swimmers." I attempted a pathetic smile for him. When Riaan was this angry, it didn't matter what I said because he looked at me like this was all my fault again. Both of us were really trying hard at cracking a joke and being kind, but sometimes our facial expressions spoke louder than our words.

"My swimmers are strong like BULL." He said flexing his skinny arm, a little bubble bicep popped up, followed by a tiny smirk.

Only a desperate wife would think it was a turn on. Yes, I was that desperate wife.

"Yes, okay dear. Just when we get there, let's get in and out okay?" I said trying to stay focused on driving there and not checking out my husband.

Stupid bicep. It is funny how cancer changes a person's perception. As skinny and sick as Riaan was, I still saw the handsome, sexy man I married. I just couldn't see him the way he saw himself. On the contrary, when I looked at myself, I now saw failure. I no longer felt like my husband thought I was beautiful. After all, he came across to the other side of the world for me and I could do nothing right, it seemed, to make him happy. I kept trying and vowed to never stop trying, so anything Riaan wanted, Riaan got; including the stupid cigarettes.

We signed in at the fertility clinic and sat down. I looked around me and I saw older guys with younger women.

I promise, I didn't judge... much.

I also saw VERY pregnant women ALL over the place – there were raging hormones racing through the air, you could feel it. I saw Riaan's face turn to disgust and I followed to where he was looking. It was then that I saw the lineup of miserable looking men. It didn't occur to me at first, that all these men, in this line up, were all in fact, there to do the same thing, jizz in a cup. Riaan caught on quickly and parked his backside next to the last guy in line. They made eye contact for a quick second, nodding in agreement, and then silence again. It was like an assembly line. One guy would go in, do his thing, and then leave. The nurse would head in, close the door for a minute, and then the nurse would come out and call the next poor old chap sitting there.

In all the years that Riaan and I were together, that department NEVER came quickly. But for this instance, wham, bam, thank you ma'am. Riaan was in and out in less than 5 minutes.

"Wow, that was quick." I said trying to hold back a snarky smile.

"I was NOT there for pleasure. Whipped it out, rubbed one out, and now I am ready to go get my Prednisone and go home. Hadley, please take me home. Jerking off is ruined for me from this day forward. Right now, I am pretty upset about it," he whined.

Ha-ha, what the hell do you think I have had to do over the past months when you won't even look at me...yes rub one out, or two or three, pending on the day. But this isn't about me, it is about doing everything I can for my husband.

"Okay darling, I am proud of you. Thank you!" I said, grabbing his hand. For once, he grabbed it back and squeezed. Funny how such a small gesture can give someone so much hope.

Woohoo, he actually held my hand back!
We were both told that Prednisone causes excessive hunger so on our way back home, we stopped at good old Costco. We both figured this would be the perfect time to stock up on good, healthy food for Riaan to bulk up on. Large bag of broccoli, large bag

of peas, large bag of baby carrots, 8 peppers, and four liters of pomegranate juice.

It is high in antioxidants, which is good for cancer fighting abilities... FYI

We bought protein powder, Creatine powder, a bag of apples, 3 bunches of bananas... well you get the point, anything that made Riaan smile gave me hope for our future... $500 later, we had a full cart of nothing but fresh fruit, veggies, lean chicken, turkey, and anything that Riaan thought he would enjoy. Now being me, completely naive, I figured this would last us a week, maybe two if we were lucky... boy oh boy, was I wrong. Good thing the prescription for prednisone was inexpensive because the food bills were going to skyrocket.

The first night Riaan took the Prednisone, everything was fine. I went to bed while he stayed up and watched some TV etc. It wasn't until about 3:00 AM when I felt a ton of movement beside me. I rolled over and in the dark of the night, I saw Riaan's outline sitting up next to me in bed. Then all of a sudden...

"CHOMP, chomp, chomp." Comes from his side of the bed.

"Babe, what are you doing?" I asked all groggy and half-asleep.

"Oh shit, sorry, I didn't mean to wake you. I am just SO fucking hungry. I need to eat and I can't stop eating." He said while stuffing his mouth with something excessively noisy and crunchy.

I rolled over to turn on my bedside lamp. The brightness of the light hurt my eyes at first, but once they adjusted, I turned over and saw Riaan sitting propped up on his pillows with a large serving bowl filled to the top with broccoli and carrots and him gnawing on them like Bugs Bunny.

'Eh, what's up, Doc?' was the first thing to hit my brain in this groggy state.

I propped myself up next to him, trying to get my bearings, "So, hungry eh?"

"Mmmhmm. This is my second bowl and I have a chocolate protein shake as well," he said as he reached over and grabbed his 1-liter water bottle and shook it up a bit.

"Go back to bed my angel, I am so sorry for waking you again. I'll take my food and go watch TV in the living room. Good night, I love you." He said leaning over and kissing my forehead and headed to the living room.

This was the first sign of affection that had come from Riaan in such a long time. Of course, I knew he still loved me even when he was angry or distant. It's cancer that sucks all love and caring out of a person. I snuggled back under the quilt and slept with a smile on my face knowing that my husband still loved me. These eating habits continued for the next 10 days.

That $500 worth of fresh fruits and veggies lasted us 4 days, maybe. By the time Blake's birthday dinner came around, we were excited. The Prednisone made Riaan's tumors almost disappear and he had the energy level of a lion and the stamina of one too, if you catch my drift.

There was no quick, wham, bam thank you ma'am, but there was definitely some extra energy that was disbursed in a positive physical way. Hell yes, I got it in. Shout out to Prednisone!

He would eat, eat, and eat, and when you thought he would burst at the seams, he would eat some more. We weighed him before my brother's birthday dinner; Riaan had gained 25 pounds in 7 days. He stepped off the scale and made me step on it because he thought the scale was broken and didn't believe how much weight he gained.

NO, I don't feel like disclosing how much the scale said when I stepped on it. So please don't ask. Turns out, the stress of carrying the weight of the world on one's shoulders also makes you carry a lot more weight around your ass, stomach, and basically one's entire body. The only upside now is that I had actual boob cleavage, now that was a first. Silver lining, right? At least I was proportionately big all over.

Riaan was luckily skinny to begin with; he needed to put on the weight. I could only imagine the poor patients who have to take Prednisone for a long time.

I thought that if it was me instead of Riaan on the Prednisone, I would probably weigh two tons.

Let's talk about how HOT my husband got with this excess weight, just for a moment. He was always a drop dead gorgeous guy, or so I thought—someone you had to take a double look at; sun-kissed skin; dirty blonde, curly, beach hair; golden-brown eyes that twinkle in any kind of light; and these big, beautiful, plump, pink lips—but he was always lanky. With the 25 pounds, he filled out and gained some well-deserved meat on his bones. Bones that I just wanted to jump right onto.

Hot damn, at dinner that night...Panty soup. All night long. Then I jumped on that bone, over and over again!

CHAPTER THREE

Jobless & Homeless

When February rolled around, chemo was starting. I tried to look for other jobs, but everything was a fail. Between Riaan's constant doctor's appointments, blood tests, drug combinations, and his constant eating, each day was filled up immediately with chaos. I barely had time to think about a job outside of what I called my donut gig and airbrush tattoos, let alone job search and focus on interviews.

"So, tell me a little about yourself Hadley" The interviewers would ask me.

"I am married, I am happy. Oh yeah, my beautiful husband has cancer. But we are fighting hard and strong and everything will be okay." I would blurt out every goddamn time. It seems my husband's cancer had somehow destroyed all my intelligent brain function. I knew I should never even acknowledge the cancer during an interview but somehow it would always rear its ugly head.

"Oh, I am so sorry to hear that..." They would each say, full of sympathy, and simultaneously crossing my name of the list of potentials.

I wasn't an asset to any employer, I was a liability at that point and completely oblivious to it.

I was nearing two months without a job and the drugs that Riaan was taking weren't covered under our health care plan. I didn't have any health benefits without a job, so I was racking up almost $4,000 a month in bills, which still included those damn cigarettes. I would pretend to sleep at night all while trying to think of a way to do this on my own. It truly felt like I could no longer breathe and like I was at the bottom of the ocean with no chance of ever surfacing. I prided myself in the fact that I had been independent of my parents for such a long time. The bitter taste of failure made me hate who I was becoming and was once again making me choke.

I had no other choice but to reach out to my parents for help. My parents had always been there for me and this time, both Riaan and I needed them desperately.

"This is a bloody terrible idea Hadley! Us moving into your parents' house will kill us. We will have NO privacy; I won't have any place to heal properly. Don't do this to us Hadley. I am begging you." Riaan cried out when we spoke about it. It blew up into a huge fight between us.

He had a man-child meltdown on me – totally not fair.

"Riaan, we have no other choice." I pleaded with him.

"Get them to pay all the bills for a couple months while you look for a job. You should be working more than you are." He yelled.

Ex-squeeze me? I Z snapped and head rolled atti-tude imaginatively.

"My parents don't have an additional $4,000 a month to spare us. I wish they did, but they don't. It won't solve anything anyways. We need a long-term solution. Once I find work, we will need to find you alternative ways to get to your doctor's appointments. I can't even focus on finding a job right now. I have to take care of you and get you to all your appointments and that takes up most of my day, I am way, WAY too distracted." I cried.

My turn to have the man-child meltdown, minus the penis...it didn't work...

"My parents would give us the money" he shot back at me.

Oh no you didn't just compare my all-time amaz-ing, wonderful parents to your crazy-ass, psycho mother. I can't believe he said this. He wouldn't even let his parents know about his cancer for fear of how his mother might react and how it would affect the rest of his family. She doesn't even work unless you count drinking and your dad can barely keep wine in her cup, let alone pay thousands of dollars for your medical bills every month.

I bit my tongue, as this was one fight that would end in a disaster. Up until that moment, I had never ever been angry with Riaan's parents or resented them. I did love his parents, but I resented the fact that he wouldn't ask them for help and he expected me to carry the entire financial burden when he saw the bills piling up.   Who was I to judge, as everyone has a story and their own lives to live.

"I understand this is not what we imagined life would be like Riaan and I am truly sorry that I can't change the path we are on. I can only promise one thing out of this. That is, I love you and that I will always do what I feel is best for both of us. I was working three jobs before you got sick and now I am working only part time so I can care for you. Moving in with my parents is truly the only solution. I can focus on finding work, while they help me take care of you." I was kneeling down in front of him, my hands in his and looking up into his eyes, begging and pleading with him to understand.

"I don't need to be taken care of. I am a MAN." He spat out as he stood up, stepped over, and pushed me aside. He walked away into the spare room and closed the door behind him.

My head dropped and I started to silently cry on the floor of my kitchen. I am about to lose the condo that I worked so hard for and now, I was literally forcing my dying husband to move into his in-laws' place because I couldn't take care of him as a proper wife should.

Epic failure moment Hadley, epic failure.

Unfortunately, as much as Riaan didn't want to move, there was absolutely no other alternative. I was about to lose my home, the home I worked so hard for. But in the end, that didn't matter. As long as I had my husband, I was going to fight to keep him alive and happy no matter what. Three days before Riaan's chemo treatment started, I had arranged for us to move everything out of the condo and into my parents' house. It had taken me two solid days of packing everything up by myself. I packed from 7 AM until I was so exhausted that I was actually able to sleep. Riaan attempted to help a couple of times, but he felt it was too much for him physically and we weren't really speaking still about the moving thing. Both of my parents and my Baba and Gigi showed up with vans and trucks to help me load everything up and out. Riaan stayed in our bedroom the entire time. It broke my heart to see him so sad.

"Hadley, Hadley, Hadley, come here my babe-a." My Baba called out and swung her arm around my waist. Don't you give up! Stay strong and we love you. Now, let's go get that Riaan and put a smile on his face," she said pulling me forward with a shit-ass grin.

"Ohhh, Riaan." She sung as she slowly opened the door to what was once our room. "Baba is here to give you some Baba kisses and hugs. They always make you feel better!" She said as she snuck up behind him.

"Ha, ha! Thanks Baba! Means a lot, it's just really hard to stay positive right now. My parents don't know yet and my chemo starts in a couple of days. I am just really freaking out." He said as he turned her way.

I stayed a bit in the background and wanted to let them do their thing, maybe bond a little bit.

"Oh shit, stop overthinking it. You are going to get chemo, big shit buddy. Be a man and be strong. Know that you have all of us who love you and who are rooting for you. Together as a family, we will kick this cancer in the ass. Then, when we are all old and wrinkly, we can look back on this and laugh about how you two used to room with your parents! ROOMIE PARTIES!" She chuckled as she sat next to him on the bed. She leaned over and put her head on his shoulder, he looked down at her and leaned in towards her and rested his head on hers.

It was a moment that warmed my heart. At least someone was able to get him to smile.

We settled into my old room at my parents' place. It was tight, but manageable. Riaan and I were prepping for his chemo a couple of mornings later when we heard a knock on our door. Riaan went to open it and saw my dad standing there with 3 cups of coffee in his hands.

"Good morning guys! Hope you slept fantastically at Hotel McLeary!" He said cheerfully, passing the coffees on to each of us.

"Riaan, ready for the big day today?" He said looking quizzically at him.

"Oh, you know it Sam. I am trying to be. But, honestly, I am shit scared." Riaan chuckled nervously slurping up hot coffee.

"Hadley, you need to shower or something to get ready still, right?" my dad asked me.

"Um, no." I looked down at myself, completely ready to go already.

"Oh, well, your mom needs you downstairs. I just heard her call you."

She didn't call me. He just wanted me out.

A few minutes later, I was getting ready to hop in the car when my dad and Riaan emerged from our room. As they both walked down the stairs, I saw a twinkle in Riaan's eye that I hadn't seen in a long time. Nothing was said, no words were needed. We both waved goodbye to my parents and hopped in the vehicle.

I so wanted to know what was said. But wanted to respect the male bonding rules, you know 'Bro Code'. So, I bit my tongue and waited, hoping he would tell me what they spoke about.

"SO, do you think I get free cookies with chemo? Just like the movies?" Riaan asked me with bounce in his voice.

That is so not what you and my dad talked about. Jerk. TELL ME!

"I don't know; I guess we will see when we get there." I said, focusing on driving and not asking him the question I longed for.

"I want cookies; cookies sound good right about now." Riaan said laughing to himself.

What on earth did my dad say to you to get you laughing again?
It had been weeks since he laughed like that. And all about cookies.
I wish I could make you laugh like that again.

"There is a coffee shop in the hospital. Once you are hooked up, I will run down and get you cookies if the clinic doesn't have any." I said forcing out a smile. I was so confused.

"It's killing you to know what your dad and I talked about, isn't it Hadley?" He said grabbing my hand on the shifter and squeezing it.

"OH, MY GOD, YES! It is!" I yelled out laughing.

Finally, he was going to tell me!!!

"Well, boys will be boys, and we had a bonding moment, and that it is all positive. You don't have anything to worry about. Your dad is a great guy, pretty funny too," he chuckled. He knew that answer was going to kill me.

"Sooo... you aren't going to tell me what the both of you spoke about?" I whined.

"Nope, so let's drop it. Oh hey, look at the bird over there in the sky. What a neat bird." He said pointing out the window to nothing.

"I hate you." I said bluntly with a smile pasted on my face as I knew he was trying to change the subject... Stupid jerk.

"I love you too, Had!" He said squeezing my hand again.

Chemo, let me tell you, at the beginning is somewhat anticlimactic. Riaan had a needle in his upper arm, they connected a bag with clear fluid, he sat in a chair in a room full of people who were in their 80's, and we did nothing for 4 hours. We were anticipating Hiroshima, yet all we got was four hours of twiddling our thumbs while waiting for the bomb to drop.　And, of course, no bomb.　This time.

All the cancer books prep you for puking, hair loss, pink ribbons, and the path of 'enlightenment'...where the fuck was all that? Boredom/disappointment at its finest. Twisted right?!

The next couple of months, Riaan and I went ritualistically every 2 weeks to chemo. We sat there playing cards or watching movies on the computer for 4 hours. Then, we would go home and Riaan would sleep and I would attempt to job hunt.　Nothing overly dramatic happened either. Riaan didn't lose his hair nor puke once. We started to regain our confidence figuring we had this... Oh yeah... We so kicked cancer's ass... Boo Ya!

We had prepped for the worst-case scenario and Riaan was doing amazing. Every day his tumors would get smaller, his morale would increase, and his happiness would come back. It was great to see the husband I fell in love with emerge through the worst. I actually started to feel like he loved me again.

It was about damn time. Now that we were on the road to recovery, we had the hurdle of drug rehab... Oh yeah, that's another one of those side effects no one ever tells you about. Massive amounts of narcotics for pain lead to addiction and drug dependant behavior, which means withdrawal symptoms and months of rehab. Oh joy!

My birthday is at the end of April; and as luck would have it, Riaan's chemo was almost done. Both of us were excited because he had enough energy to plan a little gathering of friends for me.

At least that is what he promised me. I forgot that the Methadone he was on had the same effect as the narcotics, but was used during rehab to reduce dosages with less side effects. And yes, the side effects were plenty. It caused a drop in his core body temperature so Riaan was always freezing so he thought our country sucked because of the winter and told me so at every opportunity. Impotency; which, let's be real here, didn't really matter because he stopped being attracted to me and intimacy since chemo started. I was hopeful we would eventually get our groove back. The side effects I hated most were all the forgotten promises and the depression. No matter what I tried to do or give him, it was never enough to make him happy for longer than a short moment, not to mention the millions of things he had no recollection of speaking about. His memory was almost non-existent.

The week prior to my birthday, Riaan had come up to me and sat me down to 'have a little chat'.

Oh, heck yes, this birthday surprise would be the best ever. My most amazing husband is going to do something big for my birthday this year. It was the first birthday of mine that we got to spend together. I was turning 23.

"Had, babe. Are you excited for your birthday party next weekend?" He asked cautiously.

"Oh yeah, I not only get to celebrate with all my friends, but my hubby too!" I swung my arms around him and squeezed him tight. He was alive and we were going to be happy!

He grabbed my shoulders and pulled me back and locked his gaze with mine. "I am happy you are excited and I know I promised you a birthday party. But since I don't really know any of your friends or where to go, I was hoping you could help me." He asked in a soft voice.

Seriously?

"Oh. So, you haven't started planning yet?" I asked curiously.

"Oh, well yeah, I figured we could maybe do a fire outside or something. Could you let your friends know for me?" He asked, happy about his decision around the fire.

"I guess I will let them know. Is there anything else you want me to do?" I asked sarcastically. I was a little disappointed that he had not planned anything up until now. But I figured since he was so consumed with his chemo treatments, he must have forgotten and I can't be mad because he is here with me and still alive and fighting.

He completely forgot about it, another 'common side effect' I threw my head back looking at the ceiling pleading to God, Buddha, the Universe, and any and all higher powers to give me strength to not flip out and to accept this as a temporary thing. But FUCK, it was hard.

"Oh yeah, write down a shopping list of the food you want at your party. Then we can go get everything together." He said, sounding excited that the plans were coming together now.

"How about I just go grab everything we need for MY birthday. That way you don't have to worry yourself about it." I said...also sarcastically.

He didn't seem to pick up on my sarcasm, or he really didn't care.

"Oh, Hadley that would be perfect!" His eyes lit up for a moment and then he saw my disappointment.

"Had, don't be sad, we are going to get through this." He promised.

I can't fathom the fact that you can't make a couple of calls to plan a birthday party for your wife? That I need to plan my own birthday party? That I have purchased every small token he has given me lately. I have even purchased cards for him to sign and then give to me simply so he could feel like he was taking care of me. I keep telling myself that between the chemo and all the medication for pain, it is not his fault. Okay Hadley, suck it up, you are a big girl...we can get through this. He meant cancer. It was always about the cancer.

Don't get me wrong, I am not a selfish person. I'm probably the least selfish person you could ever meet, or so I've been told. It killed me to see him so tired and so lumpy. It destroyed me knowing that this disease could kill him before we could ever have a proper chance at a life together. He was constantly on my mind, I had persistent anxiety of losing him. It would haunt my dreams nightly; I would wake up in fright that he died or disappeared. I would turn over to snuggle into his body, he would turn away from me, and he would then tell me that it hurt when I touched him. I was becoming hopeless with this; it was all we talked about. When I tried to change the subject, he would get angry with me and tell me I was being inconsiderate to him.

"You don't understand Hadley; you aren't the sick one." I heard constantly from him.

"But the person I love the most is sick and I can't do anything except stand by and watch you in pain, Riaan. That is equally as bad as being sick" I would plead.

No dice. Ever. When someone is diagnosed with cancer no one volunteers to tell you all the ugly that comes with it. No one ever tells you how it destroys more than just the life of the patient. No one tells you that it can leave you destitute and feeling like such a failure. That simply breathing every moment becomes a monumental task.

My birthday came and went. I had some friends over, it was only 5 degrees outside, but everyone bundled up and persevered. Riaan and I hadn't been out in public for quite some time, so it was really nice to see all of my girlfriends. These girlfriends were the diehard girls, my soulmates. The ones that are always there for you, no matter what. Even in the past few months, they would call constantly to check in and try and bring a smile to my face.

My girlfriend Maria and I have been friends since we were 5 years old. We played soccer and volleyball together. She's tall, lanky, and awkward, definitely one of a kind. She was the girl that went from boyfriend to boyfriend throughout school. She was currently in between men. I told her to show up around 8 PM. So, what does this little bitch do? She shows up around 11 PM hammered. She texts me about 9:30 PM saying she was going to be late and not to worry, she was having drinks with this new guy she met. I told her if she was going to be late for MY birthday that she better be getting LAID. As her car pulled onto the street, you could see from the back yard police lights go on behind her. She thought to herself that she could just pull into my parents' driveway and see the cops then. She parked her car and got out as the cop car pulled in behind her.

"Excuse me ma'am, you should have pulled over on the street. You are now on private property." The officer said shining the flash light directly into her glazed over eyes.

"Oh, well, officer I am at my destination. I am at my friend's parents' house where I will be spending the remainder of the evening." She said with a shit-ass grin on her face. She spun on her heel and waved goodbye in the cop's direction. Since she was on private property, the cops didn't do anything. The police officer turned around and left as quickly as he came. Thank goodness!

"Hey BABY!" She screamed when she got to the back yard. "I am finally here, and yes, Hadley... I got laid. Thank you very much! Happy birthday you crazy bitch." She leaned in and gave me a sloppy kiss and then partied on. She later passed out in a chair while everyone partied around her.

You gotta love her.

My girl Rachelle is the most hilarious person you will ever meet; well I think so anyways. Her laugh sounds like a seal in heat. She sucks in air as she laughs, which creates this deep guttural honking sound, in which the only proper way to explain is that it sounds like a seal in heat. She was the type of friend that showed up hours before with a bunch of food and cocktails and stayed until everyone left and helped clean up afterwards. Rachelle and I had known each other throughout school, but never got close until after we graduated. She was a wandering traveller; she would go on trips all around the world for months and come home and share all these wonderful stories. My favorite one was when she hiked up a mountain in Asia somewhere, camped out at the top, smoked some hookah, and then hiked down the following day. Close to the end of her day, her knee gave out, and she tore her ACL or MCL or something like that in her knee. Needless to say, her travelling and hiking days are over. She still enjoys her occasional hookah party.

I mean who doesn't enjoy a hookah party!? Hah! I can't even remember the last time I even sort of partied. The drug and alcohol-induced parties from South Africa seemed like distant, faded dreams.

Ironically, 'these are the days of our lives' is repeating in my head.

"Riaan, can you please grab your wife a refill? Her glass is empty, that is NOT allowed on her birthday!" Rachelle dictated, pointing her finger in my direction and winking at me.

She is a keeper.

"Anything for my angel." Riaan jumped up and jogged into the house.

Wow, he actually listened and was happy. It was these little slips of kind, loving gestures that kept giving me hope and, at the same time, kept me confused as shit as to what was going to happen next. This is the husband I know and love so much.

My girlfriend Tatiana was the difficult one to please. Once you broke the barrier, she was amazing. She lived with me for a few months in the condo before Riaan had moved to Canada. She was a few years older than me and didn't have an easy life growing up. Single mom, two older siblings, and terrible choices in men. She was a tough cookie to crack, but like I said, an amazing human being when you finally broke into her circle of trust. She didn't like Riaan at all. She had listened to me for years gloat over Riaan and talk incessantly about how much he loved me. She was always so patient with me. When I had gotten to be too much, she would calmly look at me and ask me to take it down 65 notches. You had to love her brutal honesty. During my birthday party, she sat there with her arms crossed, legs crossed, and eying Riaan up and down, watching how he treated me intently.

"I just think cancer and that aside, he is still healthy enough to take care of you at least just a little. For Christ's sake Hadley, you had to even buy yourself a birthday card so he could sign it and give it to you. I just want the best for you." She would plead with me.

"Thank you, T., I love you for your honesty. We will get through this. I promise that once he is better, you will see how amazing he is. We are just going through a tough patch right now and it is really hard for him to focus on anything else but the cancer." I said hugging her tight at the end of the night.

Lastly, my family friend Melinda came through as a surprise. She is actually a friend of my parents, but through time and life experiences, we ended up becoming really close friends as well. She was like the unofficial aunty. She loved Riaan the moment she laid eyes on him.

"Good God, Riaan, you remind me so much of my amazing, late father. You know he was Dutch and you are like basically Dutch, being Afrikaans and such." she was rambling on and on.

Melinda was a smoker, as was Riaan, and also had a cancer scare in the past. She was in her early 50's, single, and never married. She was a tough broad, sometimes a little rough around the edges, but had a heart of gold. Melinda was a beautiful, self-made entrepreneur who inspired everyone in her life. She was definitely a friend you wouldn't want to piss off and she was always there for you. Riaan had a deep connection with Melinda. It made me happy that someone who was so important to our family was finally connecting to Riaan. It had been months since he had moved here, in fact, almost a year at this point. He hadn't really connected with anyone, he didn't ever have the time, really. Right after our wedding, it was cancer and it had been cancer ever since.

"Thanks for coming Mel, I truly appreciate it. Love you lots." I said at the end of the night as she was heading out.

"Oh, you come here. Riaan, get over here." She yelled out. "Come give me a group hug. I love you both" she said squeezing the shit out of us. Riaan even let out a little squeak, as it hurt him a bit.

"Oh SHIT, I am so SORRY Riaan." Melinda yelped out. Then unintentionally giving him another hug. Riaan just smiled and hugged her back.

All in all, my birthday party ended up being a success in my eyes. The important people came through, we had a big bonfire, had some cocktails, and enjoyed an evening filled with laughter and good memories. At the end of the night, after everyone left and my mom and Riaan went to bed, my dad poured us a Scotch and invited me to join him by the fire for one last night cap before bed. I was half in the bag at that point, so I agreed, grabbed the Scotch and sat next to him by the fire.

"So, how is my favorite Dasha doing?" Dasha was our weird family name for daughter. He asked staring deep into the flames.

Austin Powers movies stemmed this weird family thing; Masha, Dasha, Brasha and of course the infamous 'Fasha'.

"She is doing." I answered back, gaze fixated on the bright orange and yellow colors of the bonfire.

"You know, when my dad got sick with his brain tumor- "He started to say as I interrupted.

"When you were 18 years old right?" I barked.

"Ah, yes. When I was 18. My dad was diagnosed with cancer when your uncle was only two years old, so Gramma was busy with him and I was left taking care of my dad. I went through the same kind of stuff you are going through now. I understand it is hard, but just keep focused. It won't be this bad forever. Just keep focusing on that." His gaze still forward, sipping slowly on the Scotch.

After a little silence, I finally got the gumption to pipe up. As we sat there, the tears welled up in my eyes and I couldn't bear to let a tear fall down my cheek. If my dad could handle this at 18, I could handle it at 23.

"I got you Fash, it sucks. But I honestly think it will make everyone stronger." I managed to squeak out a smile, just as a tear fell down my cheek.

He didn't see it, perfect! I didn't want to crack in front of my dad. I didn't want to put him through more. I know watching me like this hurt him and my mom. I understood the pain of watching someone I loved in pain and not being able to do anything about it. Just sit, watch, hope and pray they don't fall apart. He would always be there if I ever fell apart. I just didn't want him to have to put me back together after everything they were already doing.

After my grandpa passed away, my dad named the brightest star in the sky after him. He always referenced my grandpa that way to Blake and me while growing up. Whenever we were scared, upset, or even just outside at night, we would try and find the brightest star, just so we could wave up to Grandpa Art.

"Do you see Grandpa tonight?" my dad asked looking up into the vast, dark, night sky.

"Yup, I spotted him the moment the stars came out tonight and I have been keeping an eye on him all night long. I think it gives me a sense of peace. It never moves." I laughed out loud, snorted a bit, and spilt a little bit of Scotch.

Whoopsie, way to hold your alcohol around your dad, you buffoon!

"That is pretty awesome, isn't it?" he sighed, while finishing the last sip of his Scotch.

"Had, babe, it is almost 4 AM, we should probably hit the hay. What do you say?" he stood up and stretched out.

I stood up, stepped over to him, and gave him a hug. One of those long bear hugs where you literally transfer energy from one another. He filled my energy back up, and made me feel a bit hopeful again.

Thank God for the Fasha.

"I love you Fasha." I whispered from his chest

"Love you too babe." He said as he squeezed me in tight.

CHAPTER FOUR

We Are Just a Statistic

So, we finally finished chemo! Yay! We survived it, doubtfully, but we did. The last day of chemo, Dr. Morris walked up to Riaan, in his comfy chemo chair, and myself, who was sitting on a stool.

It was always a pleasurable 4 hours sitting on that stool.... Ha-ha NOT! But the comfy chemo chairs were for patients only, so were the cookies and milk. Overly dramatic eye roll.

"Well children, looks like you've made it through the worst part." She said with an 'I told you so' smirk on her face and hands on hips.

"Look Doc, I kept all my hair too! You said I would definitely lose it." Riaan said running his hands through his blonde, curly locks.

"That's right, I told you that you had age on your side. I knew that was a bonus." She said high fiving Riaan.

"So, what's next?" Riaan said, popping up from his chair excitedly. He looked like a kid in a candy store.

He looks so happy and so handsome, despite the fact that he was just getting pumped full of poison. It had been months since he even looked at me with the sex eye. It was almost easier when he was living in South Africa. At least I didn't have to see him and smell him each and every day. His smell always melted my panties... ahem... sorry my heart!

"Well..." Doctor Morris started. "IF the tumors don't grow back, we will only have to do routine testing," she said frankly.

IF.... IF... What do you mean IF? My insides were screaming at her and tearing the room apart. I was going full bat shit crazy inside.

Calmly I asked, "What do you mean IF, doctor? What happens if the tumors show up again, what do we do then?"

Bitch – you better not give me anymore bad news. I didn't realize that a simple 2 letter word could carry so much weight. 'IF' is my new least favorite word.

"Well, statistically only the first round of chemo will temporarily kill the cancer, but with time it usually grows back. With that said, Riaan has been a model patient. He has shown fantastic progress with the disease. I don't think it will come back, but with that said, I don't know everything. I am just a doctor. Cancer has a mind of its own. We all have to come to understand that. So, we take one step at a time. I suggest that is the mentality we all try and wrap our heads around. Riaan, everything will be okay. We will always have a way to fight this." She said with a hard, deep glare into his eyes. The glare was so deep that Riaan even broke it and took a quick peek at me.

He looked scared and uncertain. Hell, I was scared and uncertain.

That morning when we woke up, we toasted with our green shot of kale juice thinking and believing that we had reached the end of this horrible journey, just to be told that within sometime, it will come back and that statistically it'll happen. We both knew statistically with immigration, it normally takes years to get into Canada and it indeed took us years. At the end of the day, being a 'statistic' was slapping us in the face again. We walked out of the hospital that morning trying to push a smile out and hold our heads high, but it was damn near impossible. Riaan and I both knew that every time there was the possibility of a roadblock, it was pretty much guaranteed for us. We both knew that the odds were ALWAYS against us. I always persevered with a positive attitude, but this time, it was different. It was harder to stay positive.

I wonder how long it will be now...

It wasn't even 14 days after his last chemo dose when the first tumor popped up again. Fourteen days of focusing on being happy and helping Riaan gain his strength back. 14 days of trying to enjoy each other's company without mentioning cancer. 14 days of half normalcy. Truth is, I wanted to scream from the tallest rooftop. You have to be fucking kidding me, only 14 days! My husband deserves a break for a change.

"Hadley" Riaan hollered from upstairs. "Hadley, can you please come here a minute." He shouted again.

Obviously, I ran upstairs as fast as I could; skipping every second step, then BOOM. I missed a step and face planted onto the top of the stairs.

Mother fucker that hurt. I am so graceful.

"Oh shit, Had baby, are you okay?" Riaan saw my face hit the top stair and the entire neighborhood probably heard the loud bang my body made on the stairs. He came running over, with his left arm high in the air. He reached down with his right hand to help me up.

"I'm okay, totally fine." I said wiping dust off my body and assessing to see if I broke anything important. I shook it off and looked at him standing there looking like a kid in a classroom with his hand up to answer a question.

"What are you doing with your arm? What's wrong with it?" I quizzically asked him with a bit of a chuckle.

"Oh, I think I have a tumor in my armpit. It wasn't there yesterday, but today it is like the size of a golf ball. Want to check it out?" He said pushing the inside of his hairy armpit in my face.

"Yup, there it is, isn't it?" I said smooshing my face and taking a step back. It was nasty looking.

Imagine a whitehead pimple under your armpit, right in the crease. Like a deep, nasty ass pimple all converging together in the middle with a white tip. Now, the white tip was actually big compared to a normal white head boil. It was just a bit bigger than a flax seed. After a couple of minutes of poking it and examining it, Riaan came up with the idea of trying to pop it and see what happens.

Who in their right mind would think that popping and draining a tumor would be a great idea? Obviously, sick, twisted people like us. It was like having the opportunity to take vengeance on the cancer that had taken vengeance on us. Payback's a bitch... Oh boy, was it ever an experience.

I had recently bought a medical kit to keep on hand. We set up a little station with cotton pads, the pin, alcohol swabs, Band-Aids, and some tissue paper. I cleaned off the tip of the safety pin and wiped down Riaan's armpit. The hair was getting in the way, although it had thinned out from the first round of chemo, it was still pretty hairy.

"Babe, if we are going to do this, we might as well do it right. Can you grab your shaving cream and a razor, let's just get rid of all of it before you start?" He said with a gung-ho attitude.

Yes, I know just how absurd this all sounds. Now my husband is happy and frothing at the mouth at the thought of squeezing the shit out of what we think is a tumor.

I nodded my head and walked to the bathroom. I grabbed my sensitive, coconut-scented shave cream and a brand-new razor from the cupboard. Lastly, I grabbed a little tub of water for the remains of shaving cream and hair. I rubbed a thick layer of shaving cream all over his armpit, ensuring that everything was covered smoothly and evenly before I started. As I went up to his armpit, my hand started to shake uncontrollably. I couldn't get close to him with a razor without my body doing involuntary movements.

"What's the matter Hadley, baby?" Riaan asked a little worried.

"I can't do this, what if I hurt you?" the tears started to well up in the corner of my eyes. I could feel them burn. I didn't want to cry because I couldn't shave my husband's armpit.

Seriously, woman...shave your husband's armpit. You aren't performing a vasectomy; you are simply shaving his damn armpit. Grow some proverbial balls woman!

"Babe, I am not made of glass or sugar. I am strong like BULL." Riaan flexed his arm muscles and growled, trying to hide back a laugh. "You got this, I trust you."

Are you sure you should be trusting me? I barely trust in myself these days.

"Ok, you got this woman." I coached myself. Shaking out my arms and legs a bit.

I worked up the courage and shaved the shit out of his armpit. It was nice and smooth. Hot damn, I wish I put that much effort into shaving my armpits or legs. I had gotten to the point where I would do the quick dry shave or the butcher shave. I didn't have any extra time or the energy for myself these days, my priorities were solely on Riaan.

"Ok, now poke it, let's see what cancer juice looks like." Riaan said rubbing his hands together laughing.

"This shit is too crazy, I can't believe this is happening, but it MUST be done." he continued. I really think this must be the Methadone speaking because this was a first for me to see this twisted side of my hubby. But he seemed to be having fun, so what did I know.

I took the end of the safety pin and brought it close to the flax seed sized white head. I looked at Riaan for the OK to move forward. He nodded and I pricked open the white portion of his skin on top of the lump. Riaan didn't flinch.

"Okay, I got in there, did that hurt?" I asked as the insides of my body were shaking from adrenaline and fear.

"You did it already?" He asked.

"What? Of course I did" I screeched out.

How did he not feel that? He saw me do it.

"He-he-he, just kidding babe. I totally felt it, kind of. It didn't hurt though. So, pull it out and start squeezing. Let's see what comes out." He said shaking his arm and hopping up and down. He was a little too excited for this. I, on the other hand, was mortified, but seeing him with this much zest_gave me strength to continue for him.

I pulled the safety pin out of his armpit and as the tip slid out, a bunch of water dripped out along with it.

I screamed.

He laughed.

That is not fucking funny.

"Quick, quick squeeze it!" Riaan pitched up.

I took my two index fingers surrounding this golf ball sized boil looking thing and pressed downwards and in.

I gagged.

My tummy did a black flip, I could feel the bile crawl up from my stomach, my eyes started to water. I tried to swallow my fear and continued to press downwards and in repeatedly. Clear fluid was running down his arm in a stream. He tried to keep up with it with a tissue he used with his right hand, but there was so much. The tissue paper was instantly saturated. After about a minute of constant pushing, the tumor slightly depleted in size.

"AH, OUCH! Oh, my God!" Riaan screamed out high pitched.

"Oh shit, oh shit, oh shit", I pulled back my hands, screaming and hopping up and down.

"He-he, just kidding." Riaan pulled back and laughed.

"Not funny you jerk!" I stopped jumping around like a hysterical idiot.

"Well, what do you think? We squeezed out about a third of a cup of water, what do you think that means?" He asked me on more of a serious note.

"I have no flipping clue. I guess we need to talk to Doctor Morris about it." I said shrugging my shoulders. That was all too intense for me, my entire body was shaking with anxiety and adrenaline. I can't believe I just did that. Obviously, I can. When we called Doctor Morris, she got us to immediately come down to her clinic and see her. So, like usual, we packed up our stuff and went down to the hospital again. It had become our second home by this point. We had no idea what was in store for us now.

"So, you popped your tumor, did ya?" Dr. Morris said hands on hips shaking her head, trying to control her smile.

"Well, I mean how could you not? It looked like a boil with a white head and all. How could we not try and pop it and see what happened?" Riaan asked nonchalantly.

Dr. Morris did her thing, hopped on the hospital bed next to Riaan. She groped his body all over the place, keeping a normal conversation going, like it was nothing. Riaan and I had become comfortable with her doctor style, so we kept our conversation normal, chatting about the weather or anything in regards to South Africa to help keep Riaan's mind off of her digging deep into his chest, groin, and armpits.

"Well, it looks like he has some more tumors that are deep within his body, so we will have to do another round of chemo. This will be a bit different than last time. Riaan, you will need to go in for surgery to get a Port-A-Cath put in. We are going to book that and get you in within the next couple of days. That way, once it is healed, we can use that for the second round of chemo." Doctor Morris was saying all of this, while scribbling everything down onto a piece of paper in Riaan's medical file.

"What is a Port-A-Cath, Doc?" Riaan asked quizzically.

"It is a catheter that connects the port to a vein in your chest. It is under the skin, so the port has a septum that drugs can be injected into, and blood samples can be drawn out of. This will be less painful than pricking you with a needle each time as the next chemo drugs are stronger and may cause a vein to collapse." She said nonchalantly.

Which means in Hadley terms, it is a little bionic button under the skin in Riaan's chest that connects to one of his main veins. They prick his button with a needle each time they want to pump him full of poison, or suck out more blood for testing. It hurts him less each time and prevents further damage to his veins.

"Doc, this is just too much. This is hard for me to swallow. I have been doing research about alternative pain relief methods and such. In my findings, it said that smoking pot would help me during my chemo rounds. I didn't think I needed it for the first round, but I am scared of another round. I have an addictive personality and I am scared to get hooked yet again on all the drugs that chemo comes with." Riaan asked a little frazzled. I wasn't expecting him to ask our doctor if she could prescribe him marijuana, but hey... maybe we could both benefit from this.

"I don't usually prescribe that method of treatment. But I am not stopping you from finding it and using it on your own. If it works, it works. It also can be used to keep an appetite and keeps the nausea down. You have lost a significant amount of weight since we started you on chemo." Dr. Morris started to explain.

Basically, all the Prednisone weight he had gained in January was gone and even more. Currently, he was sitting at a whopping 145 pounds standing at 5 feet 10 inches, soaking wet, with three layers of clothing on.

So... he got SKINNY! But I still saw my handsome husband every time I looked at him. He was mine and I was still so proud of him.

"Riaan, you will need to eat more this time around. If you continue to drop weight, these procedures will be tougher on your body. So, I am telling you, no, I will not get you marijuana, but if you happen to find it yourself, I will just look the other way." Dr. Morris stated clearly.

"Ok, that is great to hear." Riaan gave the doctor the thumbs up and sent a wink my way.

We had the surgery booked for the Port-A-Cath for 2 days from then. I had an interview that same morning. An insurance company that provided creditor insurance on automotive financing through dealerships. I mean it wasn't the first pick on my possible career list, but I really didn't have much of a choice at that point. My dad's friend Darren was the District Manager and suggested I take a course to help me get a job as a Financial Services Manager at one of our local car dealerships. He promised the potential for a lot of money with some hard work, that it would be a good gig, and that I would be amazing at it. This reason alone was why moving in with my parents was such a smart decision. I doubt that Riaan saw it this way still, but If I didn't have the help of my folks, I wouldn't have had the opportunity to go meet with Darren's contact, Jimmy.

Jimmy and I met for coffee down the street at the local coffee shop. We both wore high-end suits, but were surrounded by seniors in their slacks and sweaters sipping their tea.

Of course, mine was designer on discount and a gift from my mom. She knew how much I hated handouts, but she always seemed to know exactly what I needed and when and how to boost my confidence.

We sat for quite some time discussing different opportunities for my future. He was aware of my situation at home and it didn't seem to faze him at all. After the meeting, I drew up the pros and cons. I didn't know much about the dealership world, other than what the average person knows; car sales people are sleazy and liars; it is a fast-paced life style; and there is a shit ton of money in the business, like over the $10k a month mark. I figured I had enough motivation at home to do whatever I needed to do to provide for my slowly-dying husband. I was never afraid of hard work and there is nothing that I wouldn't do for Riaan.

It sounded like a desperate win/win situation and hell, I was desperate and I needed a win. After coffees, I met my mom at the hospital where Riaan was getting his Port-A-Cath put in. My mom came to most of our appointments now, taking notes and asking the really important questions that we were far too afraid to ask. She would help us plan his home care, meals, and not screw up the 15 pharmaceuticals he had to take a day and all at different times with different foods or no food at all. Somehow, she made us both feel supported and safer. We all had a feeling that this round was not going to be a walk in the park. As I got there, the nurse was speaking to my mom.

"Hi. Hi! I am Riaan's wife. Can you fill me in on how things went, please?" I rushed over to the nurse demanding information.

"Oh, this is my daughter, Hadley." My mom said pointing out to me. The nurse turned her head and smiled a big, bright, overly cheery smile.

"Oh, you are THE Hadley. I can't tell you how awesome Riaan was. He is a super-duper charmer, isn't he?" She asked giggling. "Riaan did great; he is in recovery right now. Once he wakes up and takes a good long pee, he can go home. Oh, I heard you had a big interview today. Riaan talked all about it. He was so proud of you. How did it go?" She smiled.

She caught me completely off guard and it both-ered me that she was so fucking cheery, but she ac-tually cared, so HOW could I hate her? And besides, she said Riaan was proud of me so she definitely brings out the best in my man.

"Oh, it went really well. I have a good feeling about this opportunity." I forced out a smile.

"WONDEFUL!" she squealed out and gave me a big hug.

I stood there like a stiff piece of wood as she squeezed the shit out of me. I may have peed a little too.

Seriously. What. The. Fuck. Please let me go.

My mom sat there chuckling to herself, she could totally read my face. I didn't want hugs from a stranger, I wanted my husband to be well and come home.

I would totally accept a bear hug from Riaan though, just not strangers at this moment.

A little while later, Riaan had woken up, so both my mom and I walked into his room. He was propped up on a bunch of pillows with a plate of food on his lap and surrounded by nurses laughing, giggling and pampering him.

"HEYYYYY, there is my HOT, sexy wifey poo." He said as his arms shot up in the air.

"Hi there." I said a little unsure of what was going on.

"Babe, Babe, Babe, these nurses are the BEST, they brought me grape Jell-O. They also said I have to pee before I can go home. So, I figured I would fill myself up on this amazing, amazing, AMAZING grape JELL-O and then I can take a pee and then you can take my skinny ass home, OK?" He asked while whipping his hands back and forth, Jell-O flying everywhere.

"Ah, he is still a little happy from the drugs, but we figured his happiness was too contagious not to share." One of the nurses said while fluffing his pil-low.

"Oh, thank you Doris, you are just so splendid. Shame, you are a total peach." Riaan gave her a glossed over smile.

"Hey, my baby, come here and give your hubby a fat, juicy kiss!" he reached out with his arms, puckered up, and shut his eyes.

He sat like that until I walked across the room and gave him a soft kiss on his puckered out, juicy lips.

The nurses cheered and awed at us.

"SEE, I told you these nurses were awesome. They just love us so much. Our LOVE will PRE-VAIL." Riaan shouted out and pumped his fist in the air.

He was so high off his drugs, he was hilarious. It warmed my heart though, because I knew at this moment, he wasn't in any pain, he had no fear, no anger, and he was completely engulfed in happiness for the moment. This was one of the last happy moments we were about to have. Unfortunately, you can't see what the future holds and we didn't have any clue what was about to happen. Needless to say, there was no way to prepare for what came next.

CHAPTER FIVE

Car Guys & Blood Thinners

A couple days after we got him home from his Port-A-Cath surgery, chemo round two started. We both woke up that morning dreading round two. We figured since we went through one round already, that we were pros and that we knew exactly what to expect. We walk into the clinic and, once again, we are the youngest ones there. We sit down, Riaan gets pricked, we sit and wait for the bag of medicine to empty into his body, we go home, he sleeps for a few days, and then start it all over again... or so we thought.

Well... that is not what happens in the real world and I wish I had my big girl panties on that day. We walked into the clinic to see that everyone that we had met during round one wasn't there anymore. All the familiar faces of the patients and their enduring, kind partners weren't there. It had been less than a month and all new faces. We asked one of the main nurses about a couple of the people we used to see. She looked down and softly shook her head. A small handful had passed away within the last few weeks.

"It has been a tough month for our patients here," she said softly.

Did someone just punch me in the stomach? Literally eight people had died in this clinic within the last month. That was a hard pill to swallow, metaphorically speaking. But literally, I wish I could swallow a pill to make it all easier to handle. I was just grateful that Riaan did not hear her.

So right off the bat, this round started differently. We sat there somber and silent, waiting and watching the bag of chemo empty through his new Port-

A-Cath. We barely made it out of the parking lot on the way home before Riaan begged me to pull over. He swung open the car door in the middle of the street and threw up violently. Some bimbo drove up behind us and was blowing her horn. As the loud screech of the horn ripped into my ears, it made Riaan moan in pain and keel over again. He retched down the inside of the door and all over the inside of the car. I rolled down my window and waved the car to go around me. As the young woman passed, she flipped me the bird and mouthed at me to get my ass out of the way. If she only knew. She must have been around the same age as me, blowing her horn, cursing and swearing at me, while I watched my husband puke up his guts. It was a moment of realization that I was in this battle alone. How could someone my age ever understand or empathize with what I was going through when I felt helpless and alone most of the time? To them, I was just in the way, a roadblock they weren't willing to stop and help out.

The days after his first dose of chemo were horrible. All he did was vomit and moan in pain. The shivers he would get at night got worse and were persistent throughout the entire day. He was in constant pain and when he wasn't in pain, he was vomiting. He was vomiting from the chemo and could not keep down the pain medication, so on top of everything else, he was suffering from narcotic withdrawal symptoms. I felt like I was going through life in a fog, never really awake and never really asleep.

We had taken Dr. Morris' advice and found marijuana through my brother. Blake had a good connection for us and ensured that we constantly had fresh, safe green on us. Riaan and I would smoke it daily. He smoked it to try to keep food down and keep an appetite. It worked a little for him. I utilized it to keep my calm on. I had to watch Riaan around the clock so my nerves and anxiety were out of control and I couldn't crack in front of Riaan, my brother, or my parents. I put on a strong face in order to keep the family calm and happy, while inside I was a complete disaster. I was consumed with guilt that I put all of this responsibility on my parents. I felt like a failure, watching my husband slowly disintegrate. No matter what I did, the medical bills kept piling up and I was too ashamed to let my parents know. The pot was a moment of calm and peace in my life and helped me keep it together, just enough to plug along through another day.

It was late spring now and I had started the Financial Services Manger course through my dad's friend, Darren. Riaan had settled a bit after his first dose of this second round of chemo treatments. Each day he was slowly getting better. It wasn't anything like the first round, we were so unprepared. The course I was taking was intense but super fun compared to being on cancer watch. I was learning a lot and making some really cool, new friends. The last day of the course, my new friends Edward, James, and I were sitting at the lunch table shooting the shit about their dealerships and how much they enjoy their jobs. They were funny, they were arguing over which of their dealerships would benefit more from having me on their team.

"You are sexy and smart... girl we would totally love to have you there." Edward chuckled waving off James.

"Edward, you know that the Honda dealership doesn't need another Financial Manager right now.

Nissan would love to have you Hadley." James said winking at me.

I just chuckled to myself, as it had been roughly 5 months since I had worked full time. I was enjoying having a conversation that didn't revolve around cancer, blood work, or test results. For once, we were talking future plans, in a positive way. I wasn't prepping myself for the worst.

"Oh boys, don't be fighting over me just yet! I have to still interview at the dealerships after we finish this course. PLUS, they said I would have to sell cars for a bit. Sweet Lord help me get through that!" I laughed out loud while sipping my iced tea.

This is nice...having a conversation with adults about something OTHER than CANCER and DYING. Is this what normal life used to be like? How did I not enjoy normal conversation this much before? I can't believe I'm sitting in a restaurant sipping iced tea... Oh the simple things in life are so marvelous. I can't believe how consumed our lives had been with cancer, sickness and a constant fear of losing my husband forever.

"Your hubby is a lucky guy Hadley, not everyone would stay by his side in his case. You are a true inspiration. I hope that one day, I find someone who loves me as much as you love Riaan." Edward said patting me on the shoulder while taking a whopping bite of his sandwich.

"Yeah, buddy...it is pretty impressive. I am kinda envious of the love you have for him. He is a lucky dude." James said almost shamefully looking down at his plate of untouched food.

"Awww, thanks guys, I try. I just don't see any other option but to do whatever I can to keep him alive. He did, in fact, move to the other side of the world to be with me. So, I feel like I owe him at least that. Besides, I still think he is drop dead gorgeous and I love him... nothing will change that fact. James, why aren't you touching your food?" I asked cheerfully.

"Ah, I don't know, I lost my appetite. Every day I see you here, with a smile on your face, and such eagerness to learn and provide. It makes me second guess a lot of things and people in my life. Your love is so honest and unwavering. I know I sound sappy and shit, but seriously, I wish I could find a girl half as amazing as you are." James said softly.

Then Edward piped in, "James, grow some balls. Hadley is awesome, we don't need to bog her down with emotional shit during lunch." As he finished, he forced the last bit of the sandwich in his mouth. It was so big; he could barely close his mouth around it.

"Say chubby bunny, say chubby bunny, right now Edward." I chimed. His mouth was so full, he tried to say it, but all he did was spit out some tomato and chunks of bread.

Table manners didn't exist with these guys. Terrible, but hilarious. These two guys were definitely helping me to regain my confidence. I hadn't realized that I even needed a boost.

Just as we were finishing up lunch that day, I got a phone call from my mom. I ignored it of course, I was working and trying to portray a professional, even if faked, impression of myself.

Even though I was an emotional basket case.

A few seconds after, the missed call notice popped up on my phone and a text from my mom came through. 'Call me ASAP please ☺'

Shit balls. What now?

I politely excused myself from the restaurant where we ate lunch each day. I dialed my mom while my stomach was flipping. She knows how important this is to me and would never ask me to call her if it wasn't important.

"Hi Hadley, how's your last day of the course going?" My mom asked somewhat cheery.

I could tell she was hiding something. Please just get straight to the point woman.

"Hi Mom. It is going, we are about to start the afternoon. It has been a great day so far. What's up?" I asked, trying not to freak out on her.

I couldn't control the sick feeling I had in my stomach. All I wanted her to do was tell me the bad news. I knew there was bad news. She wouldn't have called if there wasn't any bad news. WHAT IS THE BAD NEWS? TELL ME!!!

"Everything will be fine." She said with a fake, cheery tone.

"Yup. So Mom, what is going on?" I persisted, a bit annoyed.

"Well, there is nothing to be alarmed about Hadley, but I figured I should call you to let you know." She started, then tapered off.

"Tell me what?" I spit out over the phone. My voice had gotten squeaky and high pitched. Out of the corner of my eye, I could see my classmates looking in my direction to see what was going on.

Oh my God, this is humiliating. Stop staring at me.

"Well...Riaan has a blood clot in his chest from his Port-A-Cath, so we brought him into the hospital. He is admitted, stable, and resting now, so you don't have to come down until after your class is over." She said, pushing through as much cheery positivity as possible.

"What do you mean a blood clot? I don't understand. You know what, never mind. I will talk to my instructor and head to the hospital now." I stuttered out, choking back tears of confusion and frustration.

"Hadley, breathe baby. I know this is stressful, but this is why you have me and your dad. Riaan is settled in the hospital and I am here with him. He has his own room and the Dr.'s are running some tests while he sleeps. You deserve this course and this op-portunity. Take it, enjoy your afternoon as much as you can and as soon as you are done, come here and trade off with me," she said in her calm mom voice.

Stupid mom voice. Honestly, I can't wait to have kids, JUST so I could pull the mom voice and know it will work 100% of the time on them. Okay, well I can totally wait to have kids, but seriously... mom voices .... they make you feel like everything is going to be fine when, deep in your heart, you know it won't... GRRR

"UGH" I groaned over the phone. "Fine, I will see you two at 5:30, let me know around 5:00 what you need me to bring."

"Thanks baby, we love you." My mom chirped out.

"Please give Riaan a hug and kiss for me." I asked as nicely and as calmly as I could.

"Well... I will give him a hug... but a kiss... I feel like that is crossing a line being the momma and all! He-he" My mom laughed out. "Goodbye beautiful."

As I hung up the phone, I breathed in and out deeply a couple of times. By the third time breathing in, I felt a hand on my shoulder.

"Hadley, everything okay?" I turned around and saw Edward there with a concerned look in his eyes.

"Oh yeah, um. Everything is fine." I pushed out, swallowing back tears.

"Do you want to hug? I give good hugs, you know." Edward said standing there with his arms wide open.

I managed to laugh a little, while a small tear snuck down my cheek. I leaned in and he gave me a tight squeeze.

God, did that hug ever feel good. Hugs are like the most amazing thing ever. They transfer energy from one person to another. They share a feeling that words cannot explain. They give you a sense of hope and peace, they refill you with goodness and positivity. Hugs are amazing. Anyone who doesn't believe in hugs, I don't believe in them. Crazy people.

Well, that afternoon was a complete waste of time for me. Nothing we talked about stayed in my head. It went in one ear and out the other. Nothing but the blood clot was in my mind, I didn't know what to expect or what it exactly meant for Riaan and I, but it was stressing me out terribly. I started to sweat in places that shouldn't be sweaty while at work. By mid-afternoon, I could smell myself.

Gag. Sweaty armpits, sweaty ass, sweaty who-ha, sweaty feet. Jesus, was I ever gross. On top of everything else, stress was causing severe sweating issues in my life... how pathetic!

During our break in the afternoon, my classmates were super supportive, making jokes, and trying to get me to laugh it off. I appreciated their efforts, but nothing was working. I would force out a smile, nod and chuckled when it was socially acceptable, but it really wasn't funny for me. My head was at the hospital examining this blood clot of Riaan's.

By 4:55 PM, I had packed up my books, binders, and all my papers. I was ready to go as soon as the clock turned 5:00 PM. I was out of that door at lightning speed. As I rushed out, I heard my classmates call out and wish me luck. These people were so supportive and so positive. It gave me a sense of belonging, even if it was just for a second.

My mom gave me the OK when I texted her. She and Riaan were good and didn't need anything. As I rushed, driving like a crazy person to the hospital, my brain went to all possible worst-case scenarios. His whole body turned blue, he stopped breathing, he can't move or he just dies.

I kept imagining the blueberry girl from Willy Wonka, a large swollen blue person. Will that be what Riaan looks like?

All these emotions flooded to the front of my brain. The tears started to well up in my eyes, my mouth started to water excessively, I could barely see the road. My chest closed up on me, my breathing became heavier, and it became harder and harder to focus on anything but this blood clot. Luckily, I made it to the hospital parking lot safely. I sat in my car for a few minutes trying to compose myself and push back the fear and negative emotion. I looked at myself in the rear-view mirror, I looked like a disaster. I had big bags under my eyes, a deep crease in my forehead, puffy cheeks, and acne was popping up in places it had never been before. I looked old and worn out. I was pale, puffy, and looked exhausted.

Man oh man, and I was supposed to be the healthy one.

Once I calmed myself down, I tried my best to fix my face and breathe in and out a bunch of times, trying to coach myself with confidence.

Just walk in there, smile, kiss your husband, and find out how we are going to get through this. We ARE going to get through this.
Ready, set, go Hadley, go!

I walked towards the room Riaan was put in. It was tucked away in the corner, which was nice because it was private and quiet. Although, nothing is really quiet about hospitals. There is always someone moaning, puking or screaming; machines are constantly making beeping or pulsing noises; and there is never a single solitary second of stillness and silence in a hospital. If there was, I think the staff would worry. Riaan was perched up on some pillows with his eyes closed and my mom was sitting across the room, legs crossed while on her phone looking mighty serious.

"Heyyyyyyy!" I said softly as I crossed over into the room. Instantly Riaan's eyes popped open and a smile emerged on his face.

"Hi doll." My mom whispered.

"Hey wifey, how was your day, my darling?" Riaan whispered as he tried to move. You could see the discomfort he was in and the pain it caused him to maneuver in his bed the slightest bit.

"Hi babe, how are you feeling?" I walked over softly and gently touched his shoulder.

He winced, "Ah Had, baby. Please don't touch me. I am in a lot of pain, eh."

I took a step back, shocked and hurt that I couldn't even touch my husband, I was now another source of his pain.

"It's okay Hadley, I will be okay. They said that the Port-A-Cath gave me a blood clot in my shoulder. That is why I am in pain. They gave me some blood thinners that I will have to take daily now. You know, just another drug to add to the pile." He tried to shrug his shoulders, but it caused him discomfort. He just sat there looking a bit disgruntled and annoyed with the fact he couldn't move without pain.

I looked over at my mom for some reason, maybe to get some support, or some energy, or a mom look. She gave me nothing in return. The three of us sat there silently for a few minutes, befuddled at the turn of events that happened so rapidly. The silence was painful to my ears, my brain, and my body. Just before I was about to burst into tears, a nurse walked in.

Oh, thank you baby Jesus.

"Oh, you must be Riaan's wife. Hello Hadley, Riaan has spoken so much about you." The nurse was a tiny, little, young woman maybe my age or a couple years older at best. She wore a small bonnet on the back of her head. For some strange reason, that, of all things, gave me a sense of peace. She seemed so kind and gentle and I knew Riaan was in good hands when she was there.

"Hi, it is a pleasure to meet you. I just got back from work. Are you able to fill me in a bit on what is going on and what the plan of action is?" I asked nicely.

"Oh of course. I actually just got some test results back from the doctor. So, I will walk through it with all of you, if that is okay?" The nurse said flipping through papers on her clipboard.

In unison, the three of us answered, "Yes, please."

JINX ... We don't spend a lot of time together at all, ha – JUST KIDDING!

"Okay, so as we know, Riaan has a blood clot in his clavicle, so deep in his shoulder. We can see that it is all blue and swollen around his Port-A-Cath. This is his body telling us that it doesn't like the foreign object inside of him. This is common with Port-A-Cath patients," she said sympathetically.

Oh, I see, they didn't tell us that when we got the Port-A-Cath. The Port-A-Cath was all fine and dandy when we were getting it put in. Now we have a blood clot that made my husband's body turn into a swollen blueberry. That was not on the list of things they told us! Yet one more side effect that was left out of the non-existent 'how to cope with cancer' hand book.

"So, we treat for pain and then we use blood thinners to help encourage blood flow around the Port-A-Cath. Riaan, you will need to inject yourself with one needle each day until the doctor tells you to stop. So, most likely after you get the Port-A-Cath taken out or after your treatment is done." She said cheerfully holding up a needle the size of a baseball bat.

Okay, not the size of a baseball bat, but Riaan's reaction was like he saw a baseball bat sized needle that would have to go into him each and every day for an undetermined amount of time. Holy Crap - how were we going to manage this one?

The nurse continued, "So as a precaution, we want to monitor it tonight. We will help you with the needle in the morning, so, you will be spending the night with us and if everything goes okay, you can go home tomorrow. How does that sound? Slumber party on Level 4, whoop, whoop." She cheered.

The three of us didn't react.

"I know it is difficult, to stay positive, but this is very, very common with cancer patients. I promise I deal with this almost weekly here. Hadley, we will take extra good care of your husband for you." She said patting the foot of Riaan's hospital bed.

I forced a smile, longing to snuggle into my husband's arms. "I know you will, thanks very much for everything. We appreciate all your help."

What I would really like to know is why no one ever tells you about all of the side effects that are so bloody common with cancer patients. I am going to have to rewrite the definition of common because it is starting to feel like if anything can go wrong, it will for my husband and I am getting damn mad at the world. This brings a whole new meaning to 'adulting', I really don't want to be an adult right now. Life fucking sucks.

Would you believe that the next 24 hours went according to plan? Riaan reacted appropriately to the blood thinners and drugs they gave him for pain and he slept okay that night. I woke up early the next morning with nothing to do. The course I had taken ended the day before, so, now, I simply just wait until one of the dealerships called me for an interview. I sat down to eat some breakfast and have a cup of coffee with my parents. They asked me all about the course and what I learned. It reminded me of when we used to talk about school each day. It took me back to a much simpler time in my life. I was longing for simple.

After coffee and breakfast with the folks, I made my way down to the hospital. As I walked in, I saw Dr. Morris walking down the hallway. I waved slightly in her direction. She saw me out of the corner of her eye and spun on her heel towards me.

"Good morning. How is Riaan today?" She asked snappy and quick.

"I think he's okay, I haven't seen him since yesterday. The nurse called me this morning saying he was ready to go home today." I said proud and happy.

"Okay, well I prescribed him the blood thinners. Every day he must take the injection. You might have to help him the next couple of days until he gets used to injecting himself. The nurses said he couldn't bring himself to doing it this morning. Be patient with him, but also be stern. He will have to learn to do it himself, his life depends on it" She persisted and waved her finger at me.

Wow, who would have thought that a finger wave could be so overwhelmingly powerful.

"Okay, I will be sure to keep that in mind. I am just happy he gets to come home now." I said smiling as strong as I could.

"Yup, that is good. It will get worse before it gets better. Be strong for him. You are strong Hadley; he will need you." She looked down over the top of her glasses, staring deep into my soul. "He depends on you." It was like she was speaking straight to my heart and soul. All logic left my mind.

I nodded silently as she spun on her heel again and did a little jig to a tune in her head and skipped away.

God that woman is weird, but I like her.

I got Riaan home safe and sound. All he did for three days was sleep, pee, smoke some pot, eat a bit, and repeat. Three days of peace, three days of routine, three days of small happy moments. Mostly because I smoked pot when he did and all we did was sit back, watch Futurama, laugh at Doctor Zoidberg and snack on gummy multivitamins. We both figured since candy and junk food was bad and we had the munchies that, hell, why not snack on healthy chewy vitamins. It was probably a terrible decision, but we did it anyways. At this point, who the hell cared?

CHAPTER SIX

Well I Didn't Expect That

Dose two of chemo round two was the same as dose one round two. We were smart this time though. Instead of puking on the street, we waited in the clinic until Riaan finished vomiting and then we went home. The nurses laughed at us because right after the bag was disconnected and they waved us to go home, we both sat there staring at them and in unison we both blurted out "no way in hell".

"Sorry Mary, I am not moving until I puke. I know it is going to happen." Riaan chuckled and then gagged.

Our nurse Mary was a sweet, older woman in her sixties. You just knew that she had seen a lot in her time. She was like the cool grannie that would light up a doobie with you and share all her stories from Woodstock.

Mary snickered and passed Riaan a puke pan.

Just the look of those small kidney shaped blue bowl type things at hospitals makes me laugh. Who in their right mind created a puke pan in that shape and that size? It does jack shit.

Riaan hurled into the small 'U' shaped pan. Chunks of his morning bagel went flying, landing on my pant leg and splashing him in the face. It came out with so much force, he started to laugh in between his gags. Since he started to laugh, I couldn't help myself and neither could Mary. So as Riaan violently wretched for a few moments, the three of us laughed uncontrollably between the hurls, gags, and gale force vomit flying everywhere. It was truly a moment that was only funny while living through it. Looking back, it was quite mortifying. I would have hated to be a first timer in the chemo ward and have to witness that.

Yeah... chemo not only makes you vomit but it messes with your brain and you think vomiting is funny... at least the first time.

The following days after dose two were horrible. Riaan wouldn't leave the bed; he could barely move. One morning, I woke up super early after not sleeping well next to him. His body would tremble in pain; he would moan constantly from being in discomfort. Also, a new symptom came to play, he would stop breathing.

Yup, that's right. He would stop breathing while sleeping. Seriously, you're going to stop breathing now? After we have come this far... no way in hell are you dying on my watch! I have to remember to add this to the ever-growing list of "Common Side Effects".

I would hover over him, watching him intently—watching and waiting for his chest or nostrils to move the slightest bit, hoping and praying that the next breath would eventually come, ready to pounce on him if it didn't. After watching him for what seemed like hours, I could hear the birds start to chirp outside our bedroom window. Through the crack of the blinds, you could tell that the sun was minutes away from popping up on the horizon.

Great, another night bites the dust. No sleep, no rest.

As quietly and as softly as I could, I rolled out of bed, trying not to move or shake anything. My toes accidently brushed his feet, his faced wrinkled up in pain and a small moan came from his mouth.

At least he is breathing. Some days, I would have to hold a mirror to his nostrils just to be sure, as his breaths were so shallow. How on earth did we ever get here and how are we ever going to survive?

Riaan's injections ran me about $3,000 a month on top of every other medication that was not being covered by cancer care. Fortunately, I had a good credit rating and Visa kept upping my limit because I would make the monthly minimum payment required. Some days, I would have to laugh at how absurd my life was. My husband's medical debt would take me a life time to pay off and I still had no guarantee that my husband would even be alive to share that life with me. Ironic or what.

I tiptoed through our room and gathered my clothes. I figured, since I was up literally at the crack of dawn, I could make myself useful and make some breakfast for everyone in the house. I hopped into the shower and decided to take one of those excessively long hot, hot, HOT showers. I felt like I needed to wash away all the stress and anxiety that was rushing through my body, not that it ever worked. As the hot water scalded my back, the thought of Riaan dying came rushing to my head. I thought for a second that it would evoke a crying fit, but I just sat there, emotionless. I was so exhausted mentally and physically that I couldn't even react to the horrid thought that was racing through my mind. In fact, nothing came to mind, just the thought of Riaan dying and me not doing anything about it. In reality, what could I do about it? I didn't have any control over what happened to him, all I could do is be by his side and hope and pray that he didn't die. The feeling of inadequacy was so overwhelming that I could choke on it.

By the time I was done my shower and getting dressed, the sun had peaked over the horizon. I walked downstairs in hopes of starting breakfast for everyone. As I got downstairs, I saw my dad with coffee cups in hand, ready to head upstairs to serve the household.

God, I have the best dad ever.

"Good morning my favorite daughter. How did you two sleep?" my dad asked cheerfully, as he passed me a cup of hot, fresh coffee.

The cup burnt my fingertips. I almost spilled it before I placed it down on the counter top. "Ugh," I groaned.

"I didn't sleep much. Riaan would stop breathing in the middle of the night. I just sat there staring at him, hoping that he would eventually breathe again. Great news, he kept breathing." I said giving him a sarcastic thumb up.

My dad walked up to me with his arms wide open. "Come here for a Fasha hug. Let me squeeze you tight." He said as he squeezed me super tight.

I let out a fart.

"Oh shit, you bugger." My dad laughed as he pulled back looking at me while shaking his head.

I put some fresh fruit in a bowl and made smoothies. I collected everything on a tray for my mom and Riaan and quietly tiptoed up the stairs towards the bedrooms. I woke up my mom first and handed her a coffee, a smoothie, and some fruit. She groggily thanked me and then rolled over to stretch or do her morning yoga in bed.

I never quite understood how someone could bend and stretch while under blankets and wrapped in sheets, but hell, it made my momma happy. So, I never asked. Crazy lady.

I collected my tray of food and went to our bedroom. I opened the door as softly as I could. I peeked in before I walked in to see if Riaan had moved. He wasn't in the bed anymore. As the door opened fully, I found him on the other side of the room pulling out one of his blood thinner needles. He was staring at it so intently; he didn't even notice the door open.

"Hey, good morning my angel. How are you?" I whispered.

He didn't break his stare with the needle. "I don't want to do this. I fucking hate needles and now I have to stab myself every goddamn day?" he whimpered.

"Well...I could do it today for you, if you wanted. The doctors told me that I could help you if you needed to until you got used to it." I said as I put the tray down on the dresser and walked over to him. I softly put my hand on his shoulder, trying to show him that I sympathized with his pain and frustration. He shrugged me off and walked towards the bed and sat down.

He sat on the side of the bed in his blue boxer briefs, skinny and yellow in color. He lost so much weight that his Port-A-Cath looked like a golf ball sized button on his chest.

We called it his push start or his detonation button. I know, I know, it is a little morbid. But we were soon figuring out that a warped sense of humor fit right in while coping with cancer.

His ribs were protruding through his chest and back. You could start to see his scalp, as his hair was starting to thin out. He has been poked and prodded so much that his body was covered in little black and blue bruises. He held the needle at eye level, staring at it, almost willing it to disappear out of his hands. The longer he stared at it, the more his hands started to shake. Within a couple of seconds, his hands were in full tremors. Discouraged, he dropped his hands and needle onto his lap and looked down holding back tears.

"This is not fucking fair Hadley. I want to die." He cried out.

"Aww, babe." I rushed to his side, bent down in between his legs, grabbed his hands in mine, and looked up at him. "Everything will be okay. I promise." I pleaded. I knew that my promise meant nothing and there was nothing I could do but it was all I could think of to say. I had never heard him say those words before. I knew it was bad, and I knew he was serious.

"You don't know that." He whispered as a single tear streamed down his gaunt, pale cheek.

"I believe in that, and that is enough power for it to happen. Believe in it with me. You WILL be okay. WE will be okay. I promise, I will do whatever I have to do to keep you alive." I begged him, sucking back tears of my own.

He nodded silently, while wiping his cheek off. He then handed me his needle. "Could you please help me with this today?"

"Of course, my darling. I will do anything for you." I grabbed the needle and started to prepare for the injection.

I grabbed the medical kit I bought and pulled out an alcohol pad to sterilize the spot on his tummy where I would be injecting him. I knelt on the ground and prepped the needle. Just before the poke, I looked up at him to get his nod of approval.

He nodded.

I held my breath and as gently and as cautiously as I could, pushed the needle through the skin. Once it was in, I slowly pushed the clear fluid through the tube until it was all gone.

He cringed.

I pulled out the needle and covered the tiny hole with a cotton pad, while still holding my breath. I turned around on my knees to put the needle in the disposal container. As I turned back to face him, our eyes met for a split second, then I saw his pupils roll back into his head.

"Babe?" I asked softly rubbing his legs.

No response.

"Riaan?" I asked louder and patting his thighs.

His body started to fall towards me. I panicked and started to stand up to use my body weight against his. He was dead weight, his lifeless body was forcing me to the ground, but I wouldn't let him fall.

Oh, my God I just killed my husband! NOOOOOOOO!

"DAAAAAD!!" I screamed at the top of my lungs.

You could hear the thumping of feet skipping two to three stairs at a time. Within seconds, both my parents were there just in time for my dad to help me hold my husband up. They were always coming to our rescue. Riaan had fallen on top of me and was lifeless and not moving. His body weight was so heavy against mine. My dad gently pulled Riaan off of me and placed him on the bed lying on his side. My mom was beside Riaan checking him out instantaneously and trying to reassure me he was not dead... not that I could hear a word my mom said.

"You okay Hadley?" My dad asked looking at me frantic and panicked.

Fuck, don't worry about me, what happened to my husband?

"Riaan, wake up baby!" I screamed getting off the floor, clawing at the air, trying to move towards his motionless body.

Talk about a slow-motion moment. It was like one of those dreams where you can see the surface of the water as you are kicking up from the bottom but you can never get to the air.

My dad helped me to my feet and we both shook Riaan a bit.

"Buddy, Riaan. You gotta wake up." My dad said patting his shoulder.

I sat there in disbelief at what just happened.

Did I just kill my husband?

After what felt like forever, Riaan's eyes started to flutter a bit and slowly, they opened.

Holy, fuck me. Thank God.

"Hi baby. Are you okay?" I asked; my face inches away from his.

"Hey, yeah, what happened?" He said as he slowly started to move the rest of his body.

"You passed out on top of Hadley. You okay?" My dad pitched in as my mom diligently sat on the bed checking his vitals.

"Hadley?" Riaan looked up at me broken and discouraged at hearing what my dad had just accused him of. "Did I really pass out on you? Are you okay?"

"Of course, I am okay. Are you okay?" I asked him patting his face, pushing back the tears that were ripping apart my insides.

"Yeah, I am okay. I just think the pain of the needle was too much for me. I feel okay now. Can I drink that smoothie?" He said while pointing to the tray that I forgot I brought up with me.

"Of course you can my darling, of course you can." I cried out laughing.

By dose three, round two, one would think that we would have a routine set. Well, the truth about cancer is that it doesn't have a routine, it doesn't have behavioral patterns, it isn't predictable. There was never one set path it could take, it was like an out of control wildfire, but with an attitude. We had gotten some test results back from just before we started round two. It turned out that Riaan's cancer had not only come back, but it had come back with a vengeance. His cancer now had moved into the casing of his lymph nodes, which causes the casing of his nodes to deform and crack, triggering extreme amounts of pain. With the cancer being a little bitch and the chemo breaking down his body, he was getting worse with each passing day. For the third dose of his chemo on round two, we had to admit him into the hospital. He couldn't move without being in excruciating amounts of pain and the tumors under his armpits had grown to the size of a football.

American footballs, not European footballs... just an FYI

My first interview with a local Honda dealership was the day we admitted Riaan. My mom and I went to the hospital that morning together, knowing that I would need to leave her and Riaan there and put on a happy smile to go to my interview.

"Don't worry Hadley, go kick some ass. You got this. Remember what I always say baby." She said winking at me.

"Chin up, tits out, Momma." I said forcing out a smile. All I wanted to do was cry, but I needed this job for my husband's sake.

"That's right my angel. Chin up, tits out! Exude confidence even when you don't feel it. Fake it until you make it. You got this babe. I can feel it in my bones." She said laughing at herself.

She was trying really hard to give me confidence. I wish it helped the slightest but this time it didn't.

I drove across the city and found myself in the Honda parking lot. I looked at myself in the rear-view mirror. Coaching myself, out loud I would repeat chin up tits out, like a mantra. "Girl, you got this." I shook my head, took a deep breath and walked into the dealership. One-step in the front doors and I had five sales guys all within my personal space.

"Hi there, how's it going today miss? Beautiful day isn't it?"

AHHHHHH – get out of my space!!!

"Hi! I am looking for Derrick Zeplak, I have a meeting with him in 10 minutes." I said scanning the sales floor for any of the guys I met at the Financial Services Manager course.

"Ohhhhh," they all said in unison.

I smiled.

One Filipino guy, maybe my age, introduced himself as Andre. "But you can totally call me Dre. Derrick is a cool guy; you'll really like him. I have been working under him for a while now." He said very eagerly while walking me towards his office.

"Thanks Dre. Much appreciated." I said smiling. I like this place already.

"Yo, boss man. This, uh, girl...shit. Sorry, I didn't catch your name," Dre said while holding out his hand for me to shake it.

"Uh..." I stumbled on my words and had to clear my throat. "Uh, Hadley. The pleasure is all mine. Thanks Dre." I said smiling and shaking his hand.

"Yeah boss, this is Hadley." Dre said pointing at me while bobbing his head.

"Yup, got that buddy. Hi Hadley, it is nice to finally meet you." Derrick said standing up from behind his desk walking towards me. He was a big, burley guy, Ukrainian blood through and through, with a shaved head—to hide the balding pattern thing that was happening at the back—and a nice, thick beard that was sprinkled with salt and pepper.

He stuck out his hand for me to shake it. Once my hand met his, he gave it a good squeeze.

Is it just me or can a handshake make or break a first impression? This was a good first impression.

"Please, sit down, let's chat. Dre, please close the door for us. Thanks!" Derrick said while pointing at the chair for me to park in.

"So, I have heard fantastic things about you miss." He said smiling eagerly.

We spoke intently about my course of action and potential roadmap at the dealership. The job was mine, as long as I started at the bottom and worked my way up to the position I just took the course for. Derrick assured me that it would be roughly a year of good performance on the sales floor and that I would be well on my way to achieve my professional goals. It was a great meeting. Derrick gave me confidence without overwhelming me, he gave me hope, and he even took note of my personal situation.

"Hadley, lastly, I just wanted to say that I think what you are doing for your husband is pretty admirable. I can't imagine what it is like to be in your shoes, but you are handling it fantastically. Just know that you and your family will be in my thoughts and prayers and also that if you ever need anything, my office is always a safe place." Derrick said with kind eyes.

Is it appropriate to cry happy tears in front of a new boss? Shit, don't cry, don't cry, don't cry.

I stood up, took a deep breath and reached my hand towards his. "Thank you Derrick, I am beyond grateful for this opportunity. I look forward to working with you and your team. This is going to be great for everyone." I smiled as hard as my body would allow and squeezed his hand with as much confidence as I could exude.

CHAPTER SEVEN

Welcome To Car Sales

It was the day before I started my new job at the dealership. Everyone was excited, especially my parents. They were so happy that I was finally moving forward again. They kept referring to my situation as 'being stuck in a rut', so this step was big for us. A couple of days before I started, mom and I went shopping for a new work wardrobe.

"It will be your 'Congratulations! You are starting a new career gift'," she smiled gently knowing how guilty I felt for all the handouts they had given us. My parents paid for everything, and then some. My mom would even pick up all the prescriptions and tell me they were covered knowing I had no way of paying for the medication that was keeping my husband alive.

"Okay, fair enough. But it really isn't necessary, Mom. I can do this myself you know; I am a grown ass woman." I tried to stay persistent. I was trying to feel independent and confident, even though I didn't feel that way much these days.

"Hadley, my darling. Let your momma take care of you and spoil you, okay?" she smooshed my face between her palms and rubbed her nose against mine.

She loved that move, it was even funnier to her when we didn't want her to do it. She would do it anyways and snicker to herself the entire time and then purposely take a long, awkward time in your personal space rubbing your nose. You can't help but laugh, it is so ridiculous. We are ridiculous.

We went to town in the store. It was an outlet store, so we got some pretty wicked deals. I was very pleased with my purchases and Gwen was happier than a pig in poop since her daughter seemed happy for the moment.

It is funny how the ripple effect works. Certain paths in life cause a big ripple effect, which we probably won't understand until long after it happens.

After we finished shopping, we picked up some sushi to-go and headed down to the hospital.

"Go play with your hubby, baby. You deserve it! Give Riaan a fashion show of all your new outfits, he will be so proud. Call the house when you are ready to get picked up, your dad or I will come by." She said waving goodbye to my sushi, my new wardrobe, and me.

I gathered my things and skipped my way down the hospital hallway to Riaan's room. It was a loud day on the ward. Alarms going off, people crying, families pouring out of the private rooms, nurses running back and forth. Those nurses moved like a well-oiled machine, constantly moving, gathering information, cleaning, maintaining, and keeping everything organized. Nurses deserve the utmost respect. The shit they deal with on a daily basis is beyond anything I could mentally handle.

Cheers to all those nurses, cheers to you!

I was a couple of steps away when I heard Riaan's voice. It was high pitched and angry, so I quickened my pace while trying to stay cool, but I tripped over my own feet and barrelled into the room. Riaan was red faced and had a big blue vein pulsating in his neck. In the room with him were a fat, old, male doctor and a tiny, sweet-looking nurse, it was the same one as before with the small bonnet on the back of her head.

"Hadley, they won't give me anything for my pain. I am dying in pain here and they said I have to wait for three more hours." Riaan looked like he was ready to burst as he curled into the fetal position in his bed. I just saw him the night before and he looked so different. He looked like a little skeleton in a shapeless hospital gown.

Oh my God, there was nothing left of my husband.

"Hi, uh, who are you?" This short, round, button nosed, grey haired old man with a unibrow, who happened to be the doctor on the floor, looked over his round, cracked glasses at me, like I was the intruder here.

WHO THE FUCK ARE YOU, FAT OLD FUCKER?

I sucked in air hard through my nose and exhaled as softly as I could, "I am Hadley, I am Riaan's wife." Out of the corner of my eye, I looked at the nurse whose eyes were torn. She looked sympathetic towards Riaan and me and almost looked frightened by the doctor. "What is going on? Sorry I just got here." I stuttered out.

"Do you mind speaking to me in the hallway miss?" He snipped, while rubbing his belly and hocking back a loogie.

He was absolutely repulsive.

I was about to agree to step outside, then the door flew open and my mom flew through. She had this look in her eyes that I hadn't seen before. It was a deep, intense look of anger and distraught. I was so confused that I literally froze from fright.

"Okay, who is the doctor in charge here?" my mom demanded.

"Excuse me, who are you?" the short, fat fuck snapped.

"I am THE mom, and who are you? Can we please get the doctor in here NOW?" she said pointing her finger at him and waving it around.

"I am the doctor on th-..." he started.

"Oh, great. So, what is the absurd reason behind you denying my son pain medication? He is a fucking cancer patient. You have strict orders from Doctor Morris to keep this patient comfortable. Does he look fucking comfortable to you?" Gwen went H.A.M. on this dude.

(Hard as a Mother Fucker)

"Well, I cannot give a patient his size more Hydromorphone than he is getting already." He pulled out his chart and pointed at it nervously.

"Read your chart, it specifically says 'AS NEED-ED' you tool. I will shove a goddamn needle up your ass if you don't give my son his medicine! This is ludicrous, I have already spoken to Doctor Morris' nurse and she will be down to see you shortly!" My mom said still pointing her finger in this doctor's face.

The poor nurse hadn't said a word the entire time. She had moved to the back corner of the room, partially hidden by Riaan's bed. Riaan was curled into a ball, shaking from pain, but managed to stick out the thumbs up towards my mom. I was still frozen, unable to move, speak or even think about what just happened. The doctor looked like he shat his pants, his glasses were sliding down his nose and he had no response. Once my mom took a breath and started to see clearly again, she saw how freaked out the doctor looked and spotted the nurse in the corner.

"Thanks doctor for your time, I think we have this under control now. We will wait until Doctor Morris comes to see Riaan." She waved him out the room.

He silently pushed his glasses up his nose and walked out the door.

"Don't let the door hit ya, where the GOOD LORD split ya!" my mom muttered under her breath. "Well that certainly wasn't one of my finer moments", my mom whispered to herself as she took a chair looking exhausted.

"Thank you ma'am." The nurse said rushing over to her as she grabbed her hands and squeezed them.

"He has been doing this to Riaan all day. He wasn't listening to Riaan or any of the nurses. I only found out when I came in a little bit ago and have been trying to deal with him. I called on Doctor Morris just before Hadley came in and from the sounds of it, you contacted her too. She should be here soon. I will go see if I can get my hands on a dose of pain medication for him and find out when Doctor Morris will be here. Thanks again Gwen, he really needed that." She smiled and slid out the door.

"Momma to the rescue!" She said with her head held high. My mom took a deep breath, looked at us and while her shoulders drooped, she again quietly said "well now, that certainly wasn't my finest moment". Riaan laughed as he sat back in pain.

I was still not moving. I hadn't put down the sushi or the clothing. I was only a couple steps in the door and unable to figure out what step I should take next. Should I say something or should I put down the sushi and the clothing first? Does it matter? Take a step Hadley. Do SOMETHING Hadley. Oh shit, breathe Hadley, for God's sake, just keep breathing!

My mom threw a cotton pad at me, "so, since I am stuck here now with you party animals, share your sushi with me." She winked and waved me over to break the fog I seemed to be stuck in.

We sat there eating in silence, waiting patiently for Dr. Morris to see us. After what felt like hours, Dr. Morris burst through the door, flushed in the face and blinking wildly.

"Okay Mr. Riaan, we have some stuff to talk about. I will need you to sit up and be strong." She scolded like a grade school teacher. Riaan pulled himself up with the help of the bars on the sides of the bed. His face was red, his hair soaking wet from sweat, his eyes were puffy and tearing. He nodded when he was sitting up and listening.

"We have a few topics of discussion here this afternoon. Firstly, you have a drug problem and a low pain tolerance, this is a problem. Your dependency on drugs is worsening; you need to man up. We have a drug regimen that will help you get off the pain meds, so we have a solution. Okay? Just nod okay." She coached Riaan on. He nodded, looking down at his sopping wet sheets.

"Secondly, this chemo isn't working, the cancer is not getting better." She said shaking her head, while checking things off on her clipboard of papers and files.

"With that said..." she started and then tapered off. She took a moment to look up from her papers and made eye contact with all three of us. She finished off with looking at me for a second. I locked eyes with her stare, she looked at me with intensity and strength. "We aren't out of treatment plans. In fact, our next step is a stem cell transplant, which is our last resort. We will need to do a test to see if the cancer has penetrated your bone marrow and if it hasn't, then we will start to prep for your transplant. I am scheduling it for mid-November, if all goes well." She sucked her teeth once complete, looking at each of us, waiting for a response.

All three of us stared off into the distance and nodded in unison. She bowed in agreement, packed up her clipboard and files, and left silently.

"I am going to have to tell my family, aren't I Mom?" Riaan said empty and sounding hollow. "It is going to destroy them."

"Riaan darling, you can tell them and then when they want to talk about all the details, I can take over the conversation. You don't have to go through that alone." My mom said softly walking over to his side.

The three of us discussed how the conversation with his family would go and we made a plan to make the call the following day. We waited until Riaan got his drugs and fell asleep. We leaned in and smooched him on the forehead then snuck out of the room to head home.

"Ugh, I really don't want to tell his parents. Mia is going to lose her shit. It is going to be a disaster!" I whined grabbing the sides of my head and shaking it from side to side.

"Hadley, babe. We have to. Doctor Morris and I spoke earlier today when I called her. Riaan had texted me right after I dropped you off about the doctor refusing him pain meds. Doctor Morris is concerned about how much Riaan is dependent on his pain drugs. They are causing numerous negative side effects." She reached out for my arm and we both stopped walking.

I faced her questioning her accusations, "Well Mom, he is dying, of course the drugs will help him. We don't know how bad it is, I highly doubt he is taking advantage of it. I trust him!" I crossed my arms, upset and defensive.

"I know you trust your husband, baby. That is the way it is supposed to be. Protect him, you are doing a great job. But as your mom, we have to talk about this. We are a family and we will deal with all of this together. We have to tell his parents. We have to tell them to come here and see him. That is what Doctor Morris said. She said it will be imperative to his recovery that he has their support." She spoke calmly and very matter of fact, my mom sounded like Dr. Morris for a moment... She didn't want to upset me in anyway. I could see her compassion.

I knew in my gut that the doctor said his family should come here to say their goodbyes to him. This was our last hope; we were out of options if this didn't work. What am I supposed to do when that happens? If that happens? Did I just assume my husband is going to die soon? I don't want to think about this anymore.

Well the call went exactly how we expected it. An atomic bomb went off in the hospital room. Riaan had called his parents around their dinner time.

"Hallo, Ma. Hoe gaan dit?" He started.

Hello Ma, how are you?

"Goed goed, dit is wonderlik! Ek is okay, dankie!" He was smiling and nodding.

Good, good, that is great! I am fine, thanks!

"Mom, I have cancer. That's why I am calling to-night. To tell you about it." He started to quiet his voice and look down at his sheets.

"Ma, please..." He started, but then you could hear her start to scream on the other end. It was mostly in

Afrikaans and muffled, I couldn't understand the majority of it. We heard a brief pause; Riaan took the opportunity to take a long, deep breath.

He looked up at my mom and me, "Well, one parent down, one to go!" He forced a broken smile.

Then you heard his dad's low, deep voice through the phone. Muffled still, but loud enough to hear; "Son, is that you?"

No, you dipshit! Of course, it's your son, who else would be calling you to tell you he has cancer?

"Pa, yeah it's me Riaan. Pa, ek het kanker. But I'll be okay. Can you come visit me?" Riaan asked, the tears were welling up in the corner of his eyes.

Pa, I have cancer.

A bunch of muffled chats back and forth ended with Riaan chuckling out; "hahaha, ja, fokken kanker is n bliksem."

Yeah, fucking cancer, it's a bastard. – Bliksem is a really, really, really bad word in Afrikaans.

Riaan finished his goodbyes and then passed the phone to my mom for her part. She picked up the phone and left the room so she could do her motherly thing. I hopped on the foot of the bed, hoping he would tell me all about what they said. Apparently, they told him that he should come home and that they couldn't afford to come to Canada, let alone get a visa to come to Canada. Then his dad told him that a beer and bonfire will make him feel better.

Oh yeah, they laid the guilt trip on him about money and then underplayed the seriousness of it to a joke of beer and a bonfire. Seriously, a fucking bonfire. I have to be the hard-ass bad wife, which denies him alcohol, smokes, candy and now I had to monitor his drug intake. One phone call to them and now my husband looks at me like I'm the bad guy.

Riaan spoke positively after his call with his parents, but he had instantly become delusional. His parents had successfully convinced him that it wasn't a serious issue and that he shouldn't be denied the things that make him happy the most i.e., alcohol, smokes, candy, and his pain meds... He was happy to defend their reason for declining to come visit him.

"You know it is a lot of money for them, Hadley. They can't afford it. I will just go there after my transplant." He said with a big smile on his face.

A lot of money... they could not afford to come see their son who may die... they had no idea! I didn't like the sounds of this at all.

My mom came through the doors saying her goodbyes to Riaan's folks over the phone. She then passed the phone towards me, nodding her head that I take it. I moved from my seat, took the phone, and walked out the doors before I answered.

I wonder what this phone call is going to cost me.

"Hello, it's Hadley!" I chirped through the microphone.

"Hello Hadley, its Ma. Pa says hi." Mia stuttered through the phone. You could tell she had been drinking, her words were a bit slurred and her English was a bit of a struggle.

She grumbled a couple of things that I nodded and agreed to. Going off about how Riaan is strong and is a man, something about me loving him and making sure I'm nice to him. Then she hit me with a doozie, "Don't you dare let my son die! I will hunt you down and find you. I am not joking. You keep him alive. Bye-bye darling." Click.

I didn't even have a chance to respond or absorb what was just said to me. My mother-in-law just threatened my life. I looked down at the black screen of my phone dumbfounded at what I just heard. Maybe I misheard her, maybe she was joking. Every inch of me wanted to turn around, stomp into that hospital room and lose it on Riaan. His crazy ass parents made him delusional and undermined the seriousness of his situation, they turned me into the bad wife for forcing Riaan to adhere to the Dr.'s Protocol, and now she has the audacity to threaten me if he dies.

It isn't even in my control, and haven't I been doing everything possible so far? Should I be doing more?

CHAPTER EIGHT

Monsoon Mia is Enroute

Turns out my mom made them understand the seriousness of Riaan's situation; within 10 days of telling his parents, Riaan was released from the hospital and his mother and sister were on their way to stay with us. After a bit more coaxing, they figured out a way. His sister was in for only two weeks and his mother six weeks. Six long weeks that felt like a never-ending rollercoaster. I had been working at the Honda dealership for just under a month, it was going great. I made so many new friends and somehow managed to laugh every day I went to work. Some days, I would laugh so hard I would cry or snort—actually, most days I did one or the other. My colleagues realized that using humor was the best way for me to keep it together. Most days, if I didn't laugh, I would have burst into uncontrollable tears. It was my little heaven away from my living hell at home. I booked off the day Mia and Riaan's sister were arriving. We had planned the whole day around them landing and keeping Riaan involved in as much as possible. My mom and I rearranged Riaan's eating and drug schedules just so we could adjust his 'awake' time to spend with his family.

It doesn't sound like a lot of work, but calculating times in between pain medicine doses and all his other medicine and ensuring that enough calories were consumed to keep him functioning, was a huge task.

The morning I was to pick them up from the airport, my buddy from work, Dre, called me up. "Yo, yo, yo sister! So today is the big day hey?" he said chirpy and excited.

"God help me, yes. I am just driving around the city picking up some last minute things." I said as I zoomed through a yellow light on the highway.

"I know it is going to be stressful, so I have a gift for you. Can you stop by the dealership today?" Dre asked snickering.

"Yeah, I have some time right now I could swing by... OHHHH, what is it, what is it, what is it?" I begged cheerfully.

"Come by and see for yourself." Click, he hung up while laughing.

See why I love my job?

I had just enough time to whip around the city to the dealership and then head straight for the airport. I left Riaan at home so he could sleep until we all got back. That way, he had almost an entire day to sleep and prepare for a couple of hours of excitement. I drifted into the dealership parking lot and as I drove around to the back of the lot, I called Dre.

"Hey bro, I am out back. I only have a second though, so come here." I quickly said over my Bluetooth.

"Yeah, yeah. Okay, Okay." Click. He hung up as quickly as he picked up.

I saw his skinny frame come through the shop doors. His smile was bigger and brighter than his entire body. His smile was contagious. He was a good friend, I felt lucky to have him; he kept me sane at work.

"Yo you little B. Ha!" he giggled sticking his head in the passenger side front window, while relaxing his elbows on the windowsill. "Here is your gift, I hope Momma Mia isn't as bat shit crazy as you explain her to be." He said trying hard not to laugh and be compassionate. I couldn't help but giggle myself.

I admit that I did speak negatively about her. I have constantly told myself to be positive and that Mother Mia had many challenges in her past so I should be compassionate. Although, ever since her strange threat to me and her being able to convince Riaan that it is perfectly fine for him to smoke, drink, and take excessive pain medication, it's been a challenge... even the Dalai Lama would find her challenging. It's because nothing good ever comes when speaking with her or about her.

Dre handed me a plastic, unlabeled pill tube full of fresh marijuana. He winked, pushed himself up, smacked the windowsill with his hands and waved me off.

Now off to the airport. God, if you're listening, please give me strength to get through this. Thank you. Amen. Wink, wink! Is that how you pray? I guess we'll find out soon enough. Now where is that one hitter pipe? I have a lovely way of gaining strength. Sneaky, sneaky. Smokey, smokey.

I parked the car as close to the doors as possible and dragged my feet inside to wait for them. Part of me wished I could simply avoid this entire situation. Part of me was excited to finally have a break from taking care of Riaan. Part of me was scared shitless as no one could predict what was about to happen when she arrived. His mother was a loose cannon and could go off any second. She did just threaten my life the last time we spoke and her disturbing words were constantly haunting me. I was a bag of mixed emotions, which caused me to sweat and gave me the urge to clear my throat every few seconds. My chest felt like an elephant had just parked itself on top of me and my breathing was strained all of a sudden. I stood by the doors watching intently, patiently, most of all, nervously. Everyone that walked by was a faceless blur as I was so focused on seeing my mother-in-law coming through the crowd. I had an ominous feeling that everything I knew to be sound was all about to quickly unravel. I pasted on a huge smile as I saw Mia sitting crookedly in a wheelchair heading towards me with Riaan's sister dutifully pushing her. She had a sad, broken smile on her face, her hair was dyed red and standing in all directions. The exhaustion of the thirty-hour flight that I knew so well showed prominently.

Once we locked eyes, she threw her hands in the air and shouted at the top of her lungs, "MY Daughter, oh my beautiful DAUGHTER."

Oh dear Lord. God help me now, give me strength... at least it wasn't 'hey, I'm going to kill you'.

I smiled; Riaan's sister quietly looked at me and shrugged her shoulders. She could care less at what her mother ranted over; she looked exhausted and like the last of her patience was wearing thin.

When they reached me, Mia practically threw herself out of her wheelchair at me. Luckily, since Riaan had gotten sick, my cat like reflexes were on point. I braced myself appropriately and caught her at the right angle. I bounced her off of me and back into her seat feeling relieved that neither of us went down.

She kept looking around with disappointment on her face, once she got her bearings she asked, "Where is my son? Where is my darling son?" she started to plead. I admit that my heart hurt at that moment. I can only imagine what was going through her mind, after all her son was very sick.

"I left him at home to sleep Ma, he only has an hour or 2 a day that he spends up and awake. We scheduled it so he could spend that time with you guys when we get home." I said smiling. I was happy we were able to adjust Riaan's schedule. I was doing them a favour and it felt good to help.

"Well I wanted to see my son in the airport." Mia demanded. His sister shushed her and put her hand on Mia's shoulder. It seemed to calm her right down.

Damn, I need those powers, woman.

"Ah fuck it, I need a cigarette! It has been like thirty hours you know? Ah, shame, darling push me faster." Mia yelled out as she waved a hand in the air.

I collected all of their bags from the luggage carousel and we walked up to the car. Mia insisted that she sit in the front seat because sitting in the back would make her vomit all over this weird looking bokke.

Bokke is a truck in Afrikaans. I was driving a Jeep Compass. She hadn't seen one before.

Mia had helped herself to the front seat and his sister hopped in the back. Both of them were safely buckled up in their seats before I could even open the trunk to load in all their bags.

"Hadley, shame. Can you please hurry up? I do need a cigarette and it says we can't smoke here. Oh shit, fuck it, I am going to light one anyways, no one will see." She muttered to herself.

All of a sudden, I feel like Cinderella... except this bat-shit crazy woman has all the evil of those three evil step-sisters and step-mother wrapped up in one!
'Yes Ma'am.'

GAG!
Huge eye roll.

By the time I packed everything in the back and hopped into the car, the interior of my vehicle was covered in a thick layer of cigarette smoke. The smoke latched its hooks into my lungs and gave me a good choke. I rushed to start the car and get some airflow in there. Desperate, I opened all the windows in the car and cranked the air conditioning.

"That is just awful, are you trying to kill me? THAT air is COLD!" She screamed at me while I tried to get us out of the airport parkade and onto the highway. "How do I put this up?" she asked while blowing smoke in my face and banging angrily at the window button with nothing happening.

I should have put the child lock on, bitch!
How do you honestly not know how to press a button? I can feel a year's worth of anger at the cancer that has slowly destroyed the man I love start to bubble in my throat. It made it hard to swallow. How do you honestly fuck up putting up an automatic window? Breathe Hadley, breathe. Dear God, I have prayed for strength and this is what you give me!!! I

*can't even get a moment's peace on the way home
thanks to this selfish woman.*

On the 45 minute drive home, I tried to gently
explain to Mia and Riaan's sister just how fragile he
had become as I wanted them to be prepared. My
heart aches when I look at my husband and I see him
every day so I hoped to soften their pain of seeing
him so sick. We finally made it home, I had texted
Riaan earlier to give him the time he needed to wake
himself up, freshen up a bit, and prepare for his
mom's arrival. Monsoon Mia hit land the moment she
walked off that plane in my hometown. I knew deep
in my heart that more destruction was to come from
her wake.   Riaan barely had the strength to leave
bed let alone come down to the front to greet us, so
he met us at the top of the stairs. As we walked into
the house, he waved down to his mom and sister with
a big strained smile on his face. I knew just how
much pain he was in and the energy that it took for
him to hide it from his mom and sister. I was so
proud of him during these brave moments. My parents and our guests said very quick hellos, as everyone's focus was to get the three of them reunited in
our room to sit down and catch up. Riaan's big sister
was eager to wrap her arms around him and she leapt

up the steps quickly. It took a bit longer for Mia to get up all thirteen stairs. She gently embraced Riaan for what felt like an eternity, and again my heart ached for what they must be feeling. We had been struggling for months and this was all so new to them. They closed our door and we heard nothing as they quietly reacquainted. It wasn't until a couple of hours later they finally emerged.

The girls went straight to their room, which was next to ours, and got ready for bed. I crept upstairs quietly; I didn't want to let the girls know I was around yet. I heard nothing from our room. I wanted to check on Riaan and see how it went with them. He was curled into a tiny ball fast asleep. His skin had turned a slight yellow green color, his cheeks sunk into his face while he breathed in air with much effort and discomfort. This man in front of me was no longer my husband; my husband had disappeared within this shell of a human. For the first time, I saw my husband through the eyes of others. I wanted to be happy that Riaan had his family with him, but all I could do was cry myself to sleep.

The next day, we all crammed into my dad's minivan. Mia, Riaan's sister, Riaan, myself, and my mom all rode to the hospital to meet Dr. Morris and to do what the nurses called a common cancer patient test to see if the cancer had spread to his bone marrow. The test was called a bone marrow extraction. We were told it was one of the worst tests a cancer patient could have. Usually, they did it on patients that were weighing more than 125 pounds, which Riaan was now down to. Dr. Morris walked into the room and insisted we do the test first and then do the introductions afterwards, as she was very busy with little time for bedside manner. She instructed Riaan to get onto the hospital bed on his tummy and pull his bum out of his pants. You could see his lower vertebrae and hipbones splayed out at his lower back. She instructed him to breathe deep and to keep breathing, no matter what. Dr. Morris took what looked like a thick corkscrew— but the twisty screw part was straight—and held it in her hand. After examining it for a moment, she nodded and then placed it down on the medical tray she had next to her. She then took an alcohol pad and wiped down the middle to lower part of his back, right at the top of his butt cheek.

She attempted to be funny and tried to throw the alcohol pad in the garbage across the room. It barely made it to the other side of the bed. I picked it up and threw it out. She nodded in my direction, but still focused on Riaan. She injected a topical anesthetic in the area but explained that it was going to still be painful because he was so slender. She grabbed her scalpel and made a small incision in his lower back, causing Riaan to wince in pain. Riaan's body started trembling and his fists were white from being clenched so tightly. She rubbed his back with her other hand offering comfort while I touched his foot to let him know I was there but fear clenched my throat so tightly I couldn't speak. I prayed for strength for my husband as he already had to bear so much, I didn't know how much more he could take. I heard my mom's voice quietly and calmly talking to Riaan just the way she always did, you know that mom way of offering strength and assurance. Riaan's sister was white as a sheet and she stood frozen silently in the furthest corner of the room while Mia waited outside, as she didn't feel she could be there during the procedure. The Dr. then picked up her corkscrew device thing, put the sharp tip to the hole that she just made in Riaan, and then pushed it in deep and started to twist.

Oh. My. God.

My stomach flipped when I heard a loud crack, followed by Riaan wailing in pain. The nurse and my mom held Riaan down so he wouldn't hurt himself as I squeezed his foot and tried to stay calm. My whole body started to shake, I couldn't control it. A tear slipped down my cheek from the pain my husband felt. I had no idea that when you love someone so much you actually share their pain.

Riaan was screaming like he was being torn in half as Dr. Morris pushed her device deeper and twisted harder into his back. It felt like an eternity yet it was only a couple seconds into it when she backed off, shook her hands, and looked at us.

"I had to crack through his pelvic bone to get to the marrow. I think we should be good now," She explained to us. She attached a tube to the device and started to suck out some dark pink fluid. Riaan's feet were shaking uncontrollably and his body trembled. Dr. Morris made eye contact with me and nodded to hold his feet still.

I bent down as close as I could to his ears and whispered while doing everything possible not to let my own fear come out in my voice, "Riaan baby, you need to keep still. Please try your hardest." I then got up and stepped to the end of the table to hold his feet in place as directed.

Autopilot mode engaged.

"I can't do this; it hurts too much." He cried out. His t-shirt was soaked in sweat.

"Almost done there Rye guy. Almost done. You must stay still." Doctor Morris coached him, he obeyed.

Once enough bone marrow was extracted from him, she gently pulled the device out, covered the incision up with a bandage, and proceeded to wash her hands and clean up. We all sat there silently, not moving or saying a thing. The silence was deafening and you could hear everyone trying to breathe after witnessing Riaan's excruciating pain. It was at this moment that Mia came into the procedure room.

"Well, let's do this. My name is Dr. Morris, I am Riaan's Oncologist." She said sternly and confidently, hands on her hips staring at the girls. Both Mia and Riaan's sister didn't say a word.

"You MUST keep my son alive Dr. Morris, you mustn't let him die!" Mia stuttered out." Please help him, give him something for his pain."

"WE must work together to not let that happen. If we fight hard for Riaan, and Riaan fights hard, we can get through it." Dr. Morris said sternly. "WE must stay positive."

"Oh of course, nothing but positivity!" Mia shouted and shot her fists in the air agreeing with the Dr.

Eye roll. Oh shut up.

"Well, we will know in about five weeks if the bone marrow is cancer free. If it is, we harvest Riaan's stem cells. I will be passing over your file to the stem cell transplant team that is headed up by one of the best specialists in the world as this is a ground breaking medical procedure. So, we are nearing the end of our road for a little bit. Riaan, you must be careful with your pain drugs. Remember what we discussed, you must be strong!" She looked down over the top of her glasses at his body lying limply, face down on the bed and still shaking from the procedure she just performed.

He nodded and gave her a thumbs up.

Before she left the room, she glanced at Mia and gave her a good look up and down. She kissed her teeth, shook her head, and then left the room.

"Wow, well she isn't very pleasant, is she?" Mia blurted out after the door closed behind Dr. Morris.

"Nah, Ma. She has a strange bedside manner, but she is fantastic. Without her, I would not still be alive" Riaan said slowly crawling off the bed.

"Well she wasn't that nice to me." Mia pouted.

Seriously, are you making this about you now?

"Ma, it's fine. She is the best and has kept me alive, she doesn't have to be nice, just good. Let's just get going. I want to go home." Riaan mumbled out, trying to crawl off the bed.

You could tell that he was exhausted from the test the doctor just performed. It had taken every ounce of energy he had but he was hell bent on getting out of there. He knew that keeping his mom in the clinic was a bad idea for all. He put on a brave face for his mom, hobbled off the bed, and slowly and painfully slid into the wheel chair that was waiting. He then waved us all to leave the hospital. I let everyone walk ahead of me and stayed back in the clinic so I could get instructions for Riaan's homecare and find out what I needed to watch for. Mary the nurse and Dr. Morris noticed I was hanging back and walked up to me. Mary was always so compassionate that the look she gave me caused tears to well up in my eyes once again.

I felt a hand on my shoulder. As I turned my gaze, I saw Dr. Morris's high raised eyebrows staring at me.

"You okay darling?" She asked concerned.

"Yeah, we are surviving. Mia is a handful." I chuckled out, forcing a smile, when all I wanted to do was verbally rip Mia a new ass hole. I know Mia was as worried for Riaan as I was and I hoped her demands were just nerves, but we were so lucky to have Dr. Morris on Riaan's medial team and I was afraid to do anything to jeopardize this.

Dr. Morris pursed her lips, looked down and shook her head. "I get it, Riaan's mother is very stressed. She is not a healthy influence for Riaan, she is an enabler. You must keep Riaan on his plan for pain medication, his life depends upon it. How long is she here for?"

"Six long, painful weeks. I am okay, I work away from home ten to eleven hours a day. My poor parents take the brunt of her crazy." I looked down ashamed at the fact that my parents were looking after my husband and mother-in-law.

Dr. Morris saw the shame on my face and patted the side of my arm, "That is what family is for my dear. Use your family, lean on them so you can be strong for Riaan. He needs you most now."

I smiled and nodded my head.

What other choice did I have?

We packed everyone up and took them home. It was a silent ride home. When we turned into our neighbourhood, Mia smacked my shoulder. "Hadley, we must stop at the bottle shop. We must get me some wine." She said giggling at herself and winking at Riaan. I suggested we take Riaan home first, but Riaan simply agreed with his mom.

I nodded and pulled in. She hopped out of the car and waved Riaan to come in with her.

Seriously, you have got to be kidding! Why on earth isn't his sister saying anything? Riaan can barely move and his mother wants him to go wine shopping with her. Did she forget everything we just witnessed...Oh right, she couldn't 'handle' it, so she stayed outside, right.

"Come now my baby. Come now." She waved and hobbled in through the glass doors of the liquor store.

Riaan pulled his sore body out of the car, just to please his mom. As he moved, you could see the pain he pushed back on his face. He moved very slowly and cautiously, and she begged him to hurry up. They were in the store for a long time before they emerged. Riaan struggled through the door, carrying a box of wine and a bag full of God knows what, while Mia busted through the car door yelling how excited she was to try this new wine.

When we got home, she insisted on cooking everyone dinner as a thank you.

"Shame, you are all so wonderful, and you love my boy, just like your own. We are so thankful. I must, I just must cook you all dinner." she excitedly spat as she tried hugging my mom.

My mom laughed it off, inconspicuously wiped the spit off her cheek and reluctantly relinquished control of her newly renovated kitchen.

During dinner, Mia insisted that everyone, including Riaan, have wine. Riaan knew that alcohol should not be consumed while on the medication he was on. We all knew that. I tried to kick him under the table and he ignored it. He looked at his mom, winked, and toasted everyone.

What an asshole move. Dr. Morris had once again gone over Riaan's protocol with all of us before he left the hospital and stressed the caution he needs to take with the narcotics he was taking for pain, but somehow his mom seemed to render it all forgotten.

Later that night while Riaan and I were cleaning up after dinner, which in reality was just me cleaning, I was wiping up spills and splashes that made it to the sides of the fridge, the ceiling, and even into the family room. I honestly didn't realize that someone could cook so.... Shall we call it creatively?

I confronted Riaan about the wine at dinner later that night. Terrible mistake.

"Riaan, my darling, my angel, I know, I really do, but you know better than that. Why are you going against what the doctors are telling you?" I pleaded with him.

"These vultures can't control me. I am a lion; I am my own boss. I am a MAN." He puffed his chest out.

"Yes, you are a man, there is no doubt of that. But you know alcohol will fuck up the drugs you are taking, plus the sugar in the alcohol feeds the cancer. You know all of this, yet you are doing it over and over again with your mom here. Why are you making me out to be the bad guy?" by this time, I was in tears. I felt like I had to be the bad guy, I felt like I had to keep everything under control, yet he was making it really, really, REALLY difficult with his self-destructive behavior.

"Fuck it, fuck life. Like Dr. Morris said, we are all dying, right? Why not enjoy life a little?" he said snarky and full of attitude.

Well this conversation is over.

I nodded and went to bed.

It was late August when Riaan's sister was going home, it was also my mom's birthday. Riaan and his sister got to catch up a lot during her two weeks with us. She was a blessed buffer between Mia and everyone else. She even would get in between Mia and Riaan when Riaan needed a break. It was sad the day she left, I was really going to miss her support. She was kind, genuine, and really loved her brother. We knew that after she left, we would be left holding the bag to care for Mia and act like the buffer between her and Riaan now.

...And we thought the last couple of weeks were difficult to handle. Fuck.

What is difficult these days? Nothing came as a surprise to me. If it started to rain cats, I wouldn't question it, I would just keep going along with my day, just like I am now.

CHAPTER NINE

A Dirty Martini Turns Racist

Our friend Melinda is a sucker for birthday parties, well, just all parties in general. It gave her a good excuse to sip some wine, chat about life, and laugh our faces off, so that is exactly what we did whenever we could find an excuse to party. Since we were all in dire need of a party, Melinda organized a dinner at a lovely French bistro in the French district of Winnipeg; St Boniface.

Which every time I pronounce that in my head it comes out as 'Saint Bonny Fass' in a horrible French accent.

Riaan wasn't feeling well and insisted that Mia come out with the family to celebrate my mom's birthday.

I think it was his ploy to get some alone time. Sneaky bugger.

So, Mia, Gwen, Sam, and myself all packed together in the vehicle and drove downtown to meet Melinda. We walked in to see Melinda nose deep in the wine list, quizzing the waiter as to what their best wines were. Mia's face lit up as if she walked into a castle.

"Wow, this place is quite fancy, eh?" she jigged and swivelled back and forth on her toe and heel. "Must be expensive."

My dad put his hand on her shoulder, "Don't worry, dinner is on me tonight Mia, it's my pleasure to celebrate with all you women."

My mom caught wind of the comment my dad made, and gently squeezed his hand in appreciation for keeping the peace. I was completely oblivious; I was needing some wine to help me get through this evening. I was feeling horribly guilty that I wasn't with Riaan, and I was feeling pressured to try and keep Mia under control.

Obviously turning to alcohol immediately upon arriving was a bad decision on my part, but I didn't see any other way. It had to be done.

The waiter came around and introduced himself first in French and then in English. Mia excitedly slapped the table and giggled. "Oh I love Frrrrr-rench, it is such a beautiful accent." She slurred out trying out an unrecognizable French accent. The waiter smiled and politely bowed.

He went around the table asking everyone what they would like to drink, he reached my mom; "I would like a very cold, dirty, gin martini with extra olives on the side, please and thank you." she said cheerfully.

Mia was sitting next to my mom and blurted out, "I want a dirty martini too." She turned her head and continued to chat amongst the table.

Melinda and I decided to share a bottle, we ordered a lovely Shiraz, I couldn't wait.

The drinks came a couple of minutes later. The waiter had put the two martinis down last. He handed my mom her drink with the extra olives on the side and then handed Mia her drink. Mia looked down at her drink and then at my mom's. Then she looked back at her drink and then back at my mom's. At this point, we all noticed she was put off by something. She then looked up at the waiter and then looked at my mom's drink, "What the bloody hell? AM I BLACK?" She screamed out almost chucking her drink on my dad sitting next to her.

"I'm sorry ma'am?" the waiter stood there frozen uncertain of what was transpiring.

What the hellllllll....

"SO I don't get extra olives like Gwen? What is it because I am African? Because I am white like you,

you know!" She stammered out waving her index finger within inches of the waiter's nose.

"Oh, I am so sorry Ma'am, I will get them right away." The waiter collected his things and ran towards the bar.

Mortified, we all sat there not knowing what just happened. You could see the tables around us peaking in our direction and slight whispers were muffled. Melinda stood up, "Well, I need a smoke before I order food. Mia, come out and join me." She pushed her chair back and headed towards Mia's.

"NO, I want my olives! That fucking guy treated me like I'm bloody black...not giving me fucking olives." she grinded her teeth while visually sending daggers towards our waiter as he walked towards the bar.

Melinda pulled back Mia's chair from the table, "Nope, missy we are going outside. When you get back, your olives are going to be there. Let's go." She pulled Mia out of her chair; Mia obeyed, but not breaking her gaze on the waiter at the bar.

My dad got up from the table and walked over to the bar. He apologized to our waiter and explained the situation we were in; Reader's Digest version of course. The waiter reached out, shook my dad's hand, and shortly returned with olives and a free refill on all of our drinks. He winked politely toward my mom and I.

The ONE good thing about cancer is that it brings strangers together. We all do extreme random acts of kindness towards someone we know who is fighting the cancer fight. I was never so grateful for random acts of kindness... especially from our waiter that evening.

After a few days of Mia being with us alone, we quickly realized that she was becoming more and more self-destructive. We needed to keep her busy, not only so she could give Riaan a break, but my parents a break too. We organized that my Gramma come over and paint with Mia. Mia had always talked about how creative she was and how she used to be such an amazing painter.

As a family, a few years back, we bought my mom a beautiful art easel with paints and brushes. She never used it and it sat in her room collecting dust. She always promised that when the time was right she would use it, and that day came, just not in the way we expected it to. My mom set up her easel in the family room and my Gramma brought hers. My Gramma knew the common issues we were having with Mia and brought tea with her. She insisted that Mia drink tea while she was there in order to keep a clear mind during their art session.

That back fired. Mia had a meltdown yelling that she was more creative when she had her wine and smokes. She insisted that she have an ashtray next to her easel and her box of wine within arm's reach. My family doesn't smoke, so my parents were stuck between a rock and a hard place. She was a crazy person; do you honestly think you will win a fight with a crazy person? Or do you take one for the team and just let her do what she is going to do and pick up after her... after all... she was eventually going home.

After painting for a few hours, Mia insisted she had jet lag and needed a nap. Both my Gramma and my mom rushed her upstairs to help put her to sleep. During her painting session, she successfully got paint all over the walls, the leather couch, the table, the floor, the bar stools, and the TV. She polished off a good chunk of the box of wine and half a pack of smokes. My poor mother had a nervous twitch by the end of that day. I walked into the house after work and instead of the clean, organized, meticulously put together home I'm used to, what I saw looked like a back alley covered in graffiti and smelled like a day-old ash tray. No one was up or moving in the house when I got home that night. I tiptoed upstairs and saw Mia face first unconscious in her underwear with the door wide open and the lights on and Riaan in our room in the same position.

God help me.

I walked through the rest of the house and couldn't find my folks anywhere, which was weird because I figured they wouldn't trust Mia alone in their house. I saw my mom's head move from the bottom of the window in the back yard. I walked outside to see my mom with a bottle of wine in one hand and a big, fat joint in the other. She was double fisting quickly, taking a hit from each of them back and forth and back and forth. She barely exhaled the smoke before taking a swig of the wine straight from the bottle. In the distance, my dad was watering the plants like nothing was wrong.

Am I seeing this correctly or are my eyes playing tricks on me? My mom is smoking weed and my dad is okay with it...and no one is saying anything?

My mom heard the door close behind me and looked up. She smiled a big, fat smile and then her expression went blank.

"Sooooo..." I started, waiting for someone to tell me what was going on and why this was all so weird.

"Wanna join me?" my mom asked.

"Why the hell not." I hopped over and jumped on the double lounger my mom was parked on.

"Gwen, really?" my dad turned around looking at the both of us sucking back on the bottle and the joint.

"Oh shut it Sam, you don't think I deserve this"? My mom questioned as she held out both of her hands to show how they trembled uncontrollably. "We have an angry, unpredictable woman living under our roof. Hadley, hurry up and pass that joint back. If I have to buy this shit for my son-in-law, I am going to at least enjoy it. Stop being such a hog."

Wow, it must have been a pretty rough day.

My dad turned back towards my mom's flowers, put his hand in his pocket, and continued to water and constantly turn to check on us. My mom and I polished off that bottle and joint within minutes. I found out later just how bad the day was. My dad was simply keeping a close watch on my mom who hadn't been sleeping because, it turns out, Mia suffered from night terrors that caused her to scream in her sleep. My mom would run every night to Mia's room to help calm her so she didn't wake Riaan or myself. Every evening before bed, Mia would threaten my mom if she didn't keep her angel alive and then every morning, Mia would wake and sincerely thank my mom for everything she was doing to help her son.

Oh thank God it wasn't just me getting death threats...small victories, right? How twisted our lives had become.

About half way through her stay, Riaan had a craving for hot wings and had the energy to go out and enjoy an evening with all of us. My parents and I gathered ourselves, checked our patience level, and ensured that we were all in line before taking this woman out in public.

"We are good right, ladies?" my dad asked us, squeezing both of our hands.

"Sam, we are going to be great. Let's not order booze, to try and discourage her from ordering, and let's get in and out, and always have each other's backs... right?" she said looking at me deeply.

I nodded and my dad pulled us both forward and hugged us in tight.

Thank God, thank God, thank God, I have you guys.

We went to the pub down the street, it was close and it was safe. As soon as we got in, Mia rushed to the bar and ordered a glass of wine—be aware that we weren't even seated yet when she did this.

"Ma, Ma.... MOM!" Riaan yelled out, as she was trying to articulate in bad English to the waitress she wanted a glass of wine. She waved him off.

"Mom, no! You don't have to do that right now."

"Oh fack-off Riaan. I need my wine to take my pills." She spat out while squeezing her purse.

"Mom, why didn't you take your pills when we were at home? You don't see me pulling out my meds while I am out." Riaan pleaded with her. While my parents and I sat there staring, not sure what we should do or if we should even interject.

"Because I ran out of cool drink at home." She pouted.

"Mom there is something called water, you know that." Riaan was patting her on the shoulder, concerned, and quite frankly, being the parent to her.

"Ugh, yuck! Water will kill me. Wine keeps me alive. Ha-ha-ha!" she cackled out.

Riaan shook his head and stopped pushing.

We finally got seated and Mia pulled out her bag of unlabelled pills. She started to pop them out on the table in front of us like it was no big deal. One pill of this, two pills of that. One green pill, one yellow pill. Two square pills and three round, orange pills. There were SO many pills. She guzzled her wine with two mouthfuls of pills within minutes of sitting down. We got our orders of hot wings and for a moment it was silent. There was no small talk, there was no embarrassing gestures, and everyone was minding their own business and eating their hot wings. For a second, it was peaceful and I was enjoying a good, meaty hot wing.

CRUNCH

"EINA, fuck, fuck, fuck, Bliksem!" Mia yelled out, loud enough to stop conversation at the three surrounding tables.

"Ma, what is wrong?" Riaan softly asked in between a mouthful.

Mia rolled her tongue around her mouth and spit out a tooth, "My tooth broke man! Fuck!"

Literally, spit it out on the table. Woman, you are a disgusting animal.

"Shhh, we don't need to disturb the tables around us." My dad politely said trying to calm the table down a bit.

Both my mom and I sat there looking down at our food and shoving it in our mouths as fast and as consistent as possible, knowing that if we take a break, we will either laugh or cry. Honestly, I wasn't even sure which way my body would react.

Eat faster Hadley, eat faster!

"I didn't get travel health insurance." Mia cried out, while rolling the broken, rotten tooth around in the palm of her hand.

Eat faster Hadley, eat faster and keep your mouth shut. My mom kicked me under the table. I snorted hot sauce accidently, which hurt, but worth it to keep quiet.

My dad looked defeated when Mia said that. You could see the ideas and thoughts racing through his head, his eyes darting back and forth, trying to come up with a way to deal with this. He knew as well as my mom and I did, that if either of us pitched in right now, that we would say something inappropriate and probably cause Mia to have a meltdown in the middle of the pub.

"My school friend is a dentist. I will call him when we get home to see how he could help us out. Can you wait until tomorrow?" my dad asked genuinely.

"Mmhmm." Mia nodded while holding her cheek and pouting her lip.

My mother taught me to not say anything if I don't have anything nice to say. Right now I don't have anything nice to say. Like fuck all...

The next day, my dad and Mia went to the dentist together. My poor parents were expected to pay the bill for Mia, knowing that she didn't have a plan to take care of herself. Upon getting some work done at the dentist, which I am sure cost a small fortune, my dad's friend pulled him over to the side, "Sheesh Sam, she is a handful." He said concerned looking at my dad.

At this point, my parents hadn't slept for the weeks since Mia landed. She was a constant whirlwind of disaster. I'm sure his hair was a mess and that he had bags under his eyes.

We have a McLeary lazy eye, it only comes out when we are drunk or when we are really, really, really tired... my poor Fasha had the lazy eye that day for sure and, unfortunately, it wasn't due to alcohol intake.

"Ha-ha, well we're surviving as best we can. Can't even drink in my own house, she'll drink all our booze if she sees where it is." He said trying to chuckle while flipping through his wallet.

The dentist put his hand on my dad's shoulder, "Sam, we can square up later. Just get through this and if you need to get out of the house, my door is always open. Please tell Gwen and Hadley that too. You guys are always welcome in our home for a little 'break', okay?" He said seriously.

My dad smiled and nodded, "Appreciated buddy, much appreciated."

That night, Mia finished a box of wine and proceeded to show everyone at the dinner table her new tooth. As a result of smoking for so many years, plus drinking copious amounts of wine, her teeth didn't present perfect dental hygiene, but she was proud of the new one my dad got for her. It wasn't a pleasant dinner. We all realized, except for Mia, how bad it was when Mia showed her mouth to Riaan and he gagged. I patted his leg under the table, as he gagged again.

He blamed his drugs and the cancer on why he gagged, while us three sat there trying to control our gag reflex with no excuse, but a nasty ass mouth.

The time came when Mia was finally leaving and going back home to South Africa. The day she was leaving, she insisted that I 'allow' Riaan a Bacardi Breezer for breakfast with a smoke.

"Come now darling, be a nice wife. Your hubby deserves it." Mia said, pinching Riaan's face and blowing cigarette smoke in it. Riaan looked disgusted, but pushed out a pouty smile to play along.

"I won't condone destructive behavior, but I am not Riaan's boss. He can do whatever he wants to do." I said, unimpressed with my arms crossed, staring at her and Riaan.

"Oh yippee! Look Riaan, I told you she wasn't a hard-ass, you just got to charm her, yeah?!" She mumbled out with a half-burnt cigarette hanging from her lip. She was struggling to get out of our zero gravity lounger on the back deck that Riaan would rest in. She got one foot on the ground, then RRRIIIPPP.

That fat cow ripped our lounger.

"Oh shit! What a piece of shit sun chair!" she cursed, cigarette still hanging from her lip.

Riaan tried to help her up, but didn't have enough strength. I stood there still with my arms crossed. I waited until she got up, then I went inside. I didn't want to be part of that anymore. Riaan was a big boy; he was a **MAN** in fact or so he kept telling me every time he broke the Dr.'s protocol with his mother. If he wanted to drink and smoke for breakfast before a stem cell transplant, then go right ahead.

Go kill yourself a little faster, dumbass.

I gathered my things for work and said my good-byes to Mia, which I kept short and quick and as pleasant as I could.

As I walked out the door, Riaan blew a kiss in my direction. I ignored it and slammed the door behind me.

Mia encouraged destructive behavior and made me out to be the hard-ass bitch wife. Her coming to Canada was far from helpful. I wish we didn't beg her to come. I wish we could go back in time and erase that mistake. My life would have turned out so differently if she never came.

CHAPTER TEN

Aftermath

It took a few weeks for all of us in the house to recover from Monsoon Mia and her destructive life-style. Riaan had come around and eventually apologized, realizing that his mother had manipulated him into thinking that I was a hard-ass. She had him solidly convinced that it was fine for him to smoke and drink as much and as often as he wanted while she was here visiting.

"Baby, I am so sorry. I know that you keep everything tight around here to ensure that I stay healthy and alive. I am sorry that I doubted you and took my mother's side. She is just so hard to handle sometimes." He pleaded with me one morning before I went to work. It was good to see him coming back to reality, but I wasn't sure how long it was going to last.

"Yeah Riaan, I get she is a lot to handle, but Jesus, you didn't stick up for me at all. You let her walk all over me, not to mention threaten my life every night when she was drunk. You both told me I needed to work more so you can afford to buy your own cigarettes instead of borrowing hers. I work so hard already, what more do you want? I need support from you. I have never felt so unappreciated in all my life!" Six weeks' worth of anger and frustration came bubbling up. I was not about to let this slide under the rug without making him realize what he did was wrong and that I wasn't the kind of wife that was okay being treated like trash or playing second to an unstable, crazy mother-in-law.

No disrespect to my momma, wink, wink!

"I totally get it my angel, totally get it. I promise, it will never, ever happen again." He begged me.

"Okay, I trust you." I leaned my cheek in towards his face for a kiss. He softly pecked my cheek. I turned my back to him, walked out the door, and waved. I had no energy to argue and I wasn't quite ready to move forward.

Silence is a great punishment for guys. They assume that women will go ape shit and yell and scream at them. So when we are silent, they panic... it is so great to watch their faces... yes I am evil, but I think it was validated wasn't it?

The bone marrow test results were a little delayed, nevertheless, it turned out that the cancer had not yet penetrated Riaan's bone marrow. For the first time in this entire journey, we finally caught a break. We all felt immense relief and made sure that Riaan's family all knew the good news. We were now in the clear to harvest Riaan's stem cells and prepare for the transplant. After researching and meeting with the stem cell doctor, the science behind it fascinated me.

First step is to harvest his stem cells. In order for that to happen, we went to the hospital and met a specialist. They were specifically trained to use this really cool machine to extract his stem cells and freeze them.

I know, I know, my medical terms are not totally on point and correct. But let's be honest, if I use big words I don't understand, how is the general population going to understand? So please forgive my lack of proper terminology. In fact, you should embrace it.

Riaan was connected to a machine that was similar to a dialysis machine. He had needles and tubes going into each elbow crease. The blood from his entire body was sucked out of one arm and then processed through the machine. The machine spun the blood and since each part of the blood has a different density, it would separate. This process separated the stem cells and stored them in the machine and allowed the rest of his blood to go back into his body through the other arm. It was roughly a four-hour procedure and all the blood in his body was syphoned through the machine approximately four times. This was, by far, the easiest part of the stem cell transplant. It was mostly painless for Riaan; he slept through most of it. I sat there binge watching 'How I Met Your Mother' on Netflix off my phone.

Thank God for good data plans and cheesy, funny TV shows.

Once the specialist said that enough stem cells were harvested, he showed us the bag of this half-clear, half bloody looking fluid in a medical pouch. We looked at each other not knowing what else to expect, so we nodded, smiled, thanked the guy, and left. Super anticlimactic.

Next step was to check into the hospital. Yes, I said check in, like a hotel. We had a special wing in the hospital that was specifically designed for transplant patients and treatments. Riaan was extremely worried about this process. The days leading to his check in were stressful for him. We were both so afraid but pretended to be strong for each other. We both knew this was the last resort to beating his lymphoma as all other typical treatments had failed miserably.

"I am going to be completely isolated from the rest of the world Hadley. It will be horrible. It will be like prison. How am I going to occupy my mind?" He whined the Sunday before we had to check him in.

"Well, you can read books, watch movies... etc., right?" I tried to sound excited. Truthfully, I was worried about him being stuck in a room for a month by himself.

"Babe, babe, babe...I have an idea!" He said suddenly with a burst of excitement.

"Okay, share it!" I smiled. Seeing him happy made me happy.

"What if we get a PlayStation? I can TOTALLY occupy myself and keep my brain stimulated on a PlayStation, plus we can watch Netflix on there." He got down on his knees and begged me jestingly.

You could tell that he planned this and was waiting for the perfect time to ask me about it.

I laughed and shook my head, "Those are like $400 babe. I am not selling a lot of cars yet, they are expensive. But if you feel like it will keep you happy, how can I say no?"

"Its Ok babe, Ma said she would send money for one, really think about it... you know it will keep me busy and happy. Please my darling angel, I love you so much, and this will REALLY help me." He pouted and gave me the eye.

The hey, I think you are sexy eye.
Heyyy.... Right back at ya, you sexy beast you.
Don't show him any weakness, play hard to get Hadley.
Don't. Give. In...

"Ugh, fine! You know I cannot resist your sexy ass being happy." I reached down to grab his tiny little butt knowing full well that his mom would never send a thing.

During Mai's visit, she came with me to pick up Riaan's monthly prescriptions so she saw how much I was paying every month for medication and her response was simply 'of course we will help, we're not that kind of people you know'. I knew no help would ever come but I could not deny Riaan anything knowing full well he may not survive the transplant.

"You are the best wife ever! I don't know how I ever ended up with someone as amazing as you. I am truthfully the luckiest guy in the world. I love you

Hadley, so much!" He kissed my hands, and then my lips. He sucked on them for a second. It was heaven.

Please don't stop.

That afternoon we went shopping for a damn PlayStation.

Welcome to my new sex life – video games... very expensive video games. No happy vagina.

The morning came to check into the ward, GD6 is what it was called, very official. He had his suitcase packed, PlayStation still in the box, everything was in order. Or as much order as you can fake in knowing that your husband is about to undergo a treatment that essentially kills him, but will keep him alive just enough using red and white blood cells so his organs don't shut down and bleed out. Riaan was calm and relaxed for most of the morning. It wasn't until we had settled him in that he started to panic again. We had set up his bed and PlayStation and made a nice, little, cozy area for me. The nurses came in all at once and introduced themselves.

Chris was Riaan's main nurse. He was extremely good looking, too good looking to be straight, but hell, he was nice for me to look at anyways. Lisa was the second-in-command nurse. She was a tiny, middle-aged woman with three teenage boys and she assured me that she would keep Riaan in line. Then, there was Suzy, the head nurse of the ward. She was boss lady second to Riaan's stem cell doctor. She stood six feet or more and was a strong, intimidating lady whose presence you could feel a mile away. These three nurses scared me, but they looked efficient and assured me that they would take good care of Riaan. Even Riaan seemed confident with the team he had on his side.

"Riaan, now that you are settled, we are going to call the doctor up to talk you through the whole procedure. Can we get you anything in the meantime?" Chris asked nicely. Riaan smiled at him and shook his head no. Chris then looked up at me, asking the same with his eyes. I smiled hard, shook my head no, and then did a hair flip.

Totally unintentional. I mean he had to be gay he was so pretty.

Everyone left the room. Riaan looked back at me and said, "I saw that Had, haha!" He laughed out loud.

Whoopsie

"I didn't mean to; it just came out. But, honestly Riaan, you have to admit Chris is a pretty good looking guy. At least you have a guy nurse on your team. That is pretty cool." I shrugged and laughed it off.

"Yeah, it's awesome that I have a guy around. There are barely any guy nurses around and I spend so much time with nurses these days." He chuckled to himself while playing with his pillow.

The doctor walked in. He was about 6 foot 3, and skinny. He had dark, thick hair with a bit of a curl to it. He wore a perfectly tailored dark blue suit, with a tan brown tie, to match his belt and shoes.

This is the nicest dressed doctor I've ever seen in my life.

He sauntered in, square glasses hanging off the end of his nose. He must have been in his late 30's. "Riaan, it is a pleasure to meet you. It's nice to meet another Afrikaaner on this side of the pond." His Afrikaans accent rung in my ears.

This is going to be great. He and Riaan will bond and he can help Riaan stay strong. Hopefully they click, it will make my life a lot easier.

"Ah, hey Doc, I can't believe it! This is awesome. I am VERY happy you're my doctor. Please keep me alive and kill my cancer okay?" Riaan chuckled and reached forward to shake the doctor's hand.

"Ha-ha, you're going to do great Riaan. I have all the faith in the world. It won't be easy, but you have a good support system by the looks of it" as he points to me.

I reached out to shake his hand. "Hi, I am the wife. My name is Hadley."

"What a beautiful name. Welcome Hadley and thanks for being here with us today. So, shall we have a seat and go through the next few weeks together?" He sat down in a chair in the corner while Riaan and I sat on the hospital bed together.

We held each other's hands and nodded yes for the doctor to continue.

"Okay, so tonight we are going to start the treatment. What is going to happen is, you will get seven days of chemotherapy. Each day, the chemo is different, so you will have different side effects. Our nurses are well trained and highly educated. The staff will go over each of the side effects before hooking you up every day. After the seven days of chemo are complete, we let it work its magic, and by magic, I mean the chemo will literally kill most of the living cells within your body—the good, the bad, and the ugly ones. Roughly three days after the chemo is done, so on day ten, we inject your healthy, frozen stem cells back into your body. Then, we let science do its thing. Usually days 14-17 are the hardest for our patients. By day 21, you should start to feel better and by day 30, you should be ready to go home. I know that sounds like a lot right now, but do you guys have any questions?" He asked rubbing his hands together, ready for us to attack him with questions.

Riaan looked at me quizzically, I think hoping that I had some questions for the doctor, although I was rendered speechless. He had just offloaded so much information; I didn't know where to start.

"So, I can come and visit him throughout this entire process, right?" I asked abruptly.

"As long as Riaan wants you to come, you are more than welcome to." He said smiling and looking intently to Riaan.

If he wants me to come?

"Oh, if I had a choice, I would want my wife next to me at all times, but she has to work. But, she'll be here every day, right babe?" He smiled at me while squeezing my hand.

"That sounds perfect to me." The doctor said clapping twice and standing up. "Well, if any more questions come up, here is my card. Give me a ring or an email. It was a pleasure meeting both of you." He handed Riaan the card, gave us a wink, and left the room.

"Well...that doesn't sound too bad, right?" Riaan said staring at the business card.

"I think it will be a journey." I said a bit worried, but pushed out a smile for Riaan.

Seriously... Journey... I hate that word; it is used quite often around the cancer ward... as if any of this has been a fabulous journey. The word used to have a positive connotation for me but now journey translates to a trip through hell.

Thirty days in this small hospital room will drive the average person crazy, but when you add chemo, a dependency on narcotics, and terrible hospital food, it spells a recipe for disaster. However, the doctor seemed confident, therefore I was confident. I had to be, for Riaan's sake. I knew he was okay at that moment, but the road ahead of us was dark and scary looking.

A few minutes after the doctor left, Suzy the nurse walked in with a bag of medicine and a big smile on her face. "Ready to get started Riaan?"

"I am as ready as I'll ever be Suzy. Hook me up." He said taking off his shirt to show off his Port-A-Cath.

"Great, it will be a wild ride, but hell, we'll get through it." She chirped as she hooked Riaan up to the clear bag of fluid.

It was so deceiving; the bag of fluid is clear as water. How could something so powerful and destructive look like something our bodies are mostly made up of?

"So how will this chemo make me feel?" Riaan looked at Suzy and asked.

"Well, it usually bothers the patient's head, hands and/or feet. Random I know, but you'll only be hooked up for four hours and we check on you every 30 minutes. You shouldn't feel any different for the first half." Suzy said while writing everything out on the white board on the wall.

Suzy wrote out the chemo time frame, the day, and his blood levels. She created a chart on the white board so that every day they could update it.

"This is to help keep us all on the same page. We are looking forward to day 10 and day 17. Any questions before I leave you two to have some one-on-one time?" She giggled to herself while washing her hands.

Riaan pitched up, "Nope, we are good here. Thanks Suzy. We will call you if I feel anything funky. Thanks much!" he waved her off.

"Alright my angel, let's put on a movie and chill out. Come on up in hubby's arms and snuggle me!" He said arms wide open, hooked to a bag full of chemo and a big ass smile on his face.

It was an ugly, happy moment; a traumatic, happy moment; but hell, at least we had a happy moment.

It wasn't long before Riaan started to shift and maneuver under me while we were watching the movie. I looked back over my shoulder at him to see what was up. He pushed out a painful smile.

"Everything okay babe?" I whispered.

"My head, it is feeling funny. Can you pass me some water, maybe it will pass?" He said rubbing his temples gently.

I passed the water from the side table to him and continued to watch the movie.

Another 15 minutes passed and he started to moan in between breaths.

"What is up my darling, you are moaning." I asked quizzically, pulling my body weight off of him and looking directly at him.

"My head, it is weird. It feels like my brain is swelling. My scalp feels like it is tearing apart." He rubbed his head again as his eyes started to water.

"Is it really bad? Should I get the nurse?" I asked as I hopped up off the bed and started to dart around the room looking for anything that will help.

I literally walked circles around the room, not really knowing where to go or what to do. Think Hadley, think!

"My head feels like it is exploding from the inside out Hadley. Yes, go get the nurse." He snapped.

I froze on the spot. Literally 45 seconds ago, we were snuggled in and everything was just fine and now, he says his head is exploding and snapping at me.

Move Hadley.
Nope, you ain't going to move are you?
Hell no.
My body and my brain were NOT connecting to one another.

"Hadley! Please GO!" Riaan raised his voice and it cracked into a squeak. At this point, he was holding his head with the palms of his hands and squeezing as hard as he could. You could see a big, blue vein pop out of the middle of his forehead and another throbbing vein in his neck. His eyes welled up with tears and were streaming down his face as he tried to breathe through it. And of course, I stood there and stared at him unable to move. After what seemed like forever, I walked over to his bed where he was sitting and pressed the nurse call button. I couldn't peel my eyes off of Riaan. I had never seen him go from okay to horrid pain in such a quick time.

Within seconds, a nurse came bolting through the door, "Hey you two love birds, what can I do to help?" Lisa asked.

Before Riaan could muster up an answer and long before I collected my thoughts enough to speak, she took one quick look at Riaan, "Ahhhh. Head feels a bit funky doesn't it?" she said as she walked over and patted Riaan's shoulders. "It is a normal side effect of this chemo. I'm sorry you have to go through this. I can grab some pain meds for you and then you should rest. Only an hour or so more before you're done with chemo. You'll be ready for bed soon." She said while looking at me, still frozen, gaze fixated on Riaan.

Here we go again with one of those normal side effects. I must remember to write these down and start a hand book of all the stupid fucking common side effects of cancer. Fuck cancer.

It took me a second, but when I realized she was talking about me, I kicked back into reality. "Oh me? Of course, once he is settled, I will go when he tells me to!" I pushed out a smile trying to look in Lisa's direction. It was so hard to take my eyes off of Riaan.

"Ughhhhh" Riaan let out a big moan and leaned back into the bed. He pushed his head into the pillow and moaned again.

Lisa finished writing something in a file and some numbers and times on the whiteboard and then left silently.

"Baby, Baby, listen to me. Be strong, Lisa has gone to get some pain meds for you." I said touching his shoulder to let him know I was close.

"Please DON'T touch me! Everything is in pain right now. FUCK, can she hurry up?!" Riaan whined face first into his pillow.

"Patience my darling, she will be back soon." I almost went to touch him again and just before my finger grazed his t-shirt, he shrugged and moaned again into the pillow.

He sounded like a woman going through labor, but who am I to judge. He got so angry so fast, I didn't have any time to acclimatize to the feelings he was feeling, so my fear and nerves switched to humor. Humor was the only feeling I couldn't control and all I wanted to do was giggle. It was so beyond inappropriate considering I was so scared and couldn't help my husband. On the contrary it seemed that I only made things worse.

Lisa came barrelling in a couple seconds later with a bag of medicine in her hand and a cup of ice.

"Here you go Riaan, suck on these to help with the pain." She passed him the cup of ice and then started right away on hooking up the bag of pain medicine. "This is Hydromorphone, so the strongest stuff out there. You've been on this before, right?" she asked while hooking up all the tubes.

Riaan nodded yes, still holding his head.

"Okay, so you can get this bag every four hours okay? Stay strong. I will come back to check on you in 15 minutes." She finished with the tubes and left me there by myself to watch my husband squeeze the shit out of his own head.

"Soooo, can I help?" I asked Riaan as softly as I could.

He shook his head no.

"Do you want me to stay?" I asked him.

He shook his head no again.

"Okay, I will leave then. Will you text me later?" I asked again softly and went to touch his foot under the covers.

"Please don't touch me. I'll call you later." He groaned.

I pulled my hand back away from his feet, at a loss of what I was supposed to do. I see him in distress and in pain and I can't do anything, he doesn't even want me here. I looked down at my feet, took a deep breath and left.

I didn't get a call from Riaan that night. I waited up as long as I could. I even sent him a text; 'I love you. Be strong'...

No answer.

It was Tuesday the next day, so I had to go to work. When I woke up, the first thing I did was check my phone, in hopes that I would have something from Riaan.

Nothing.

I got ready for work and as I sat in my car in my parent's driveway, I stared at my phone trying to decide how I could reach out to him without becoming an annoyance or making him think I was becoming a pest. I gingerly typed out 'I love you, good luck today' and stared at it for a couple of minutes, deliberating if it would do me any benefit in sending this to him.

It is a positive message, who doesn't like waking up to 'I Love You' text messages?
Send it Hadley.
Or on the other hand.
You are nagging and bugging him. He wants to be alone, leave him alone. When he is ready, he will reach out to you.
Don't send it Hadley.
Fuck you inner voice, fuck you.
I sent it.

All day, every chance I could get, I looked at my phone, hoping and praying that I got something, ANYTHING from Riaan.

Nothing. Again.

The day crept by slowly. Watching a snail race on the sidewalk would have been faster than how my day was going. At 5:59 PM, I collected my things and ran to my car. I had made it through the day, it was now time for me to go hang out with my husband.

Maybe he is just sleeping.
Maybe he is too sick to answer his phone.
What if something bad happened?
Hadley... stop it! Just go to the hospital and see for yourself what happened. Don't think about it, just drive.

I got to ward GD6, where Riaan was. I walked in through both sets of doors, then washed my hands and arms. Once I got my hospital jacket, slippers, hair net, gloves and mask on, I walked up to the nurses' desk to get an update.

"Hi there guys, how is the day today? Chemo day number two. How is my hubby?" I asked nervously, trying to smile and laugh through it all.

"OH, hi Hadley, did Riaan not call you today?" Chris, the male nurse asked me, looking concerned to see me.

Uh oh.

"No, he didn't!" I said a little perturbed. "Was he supposed to?" I continued, my voice cracked and started to shake a bit.

"Oh, nothing to be alarmed about. He had mentioned he wasn't up for visitors today. That's all, but if he didn't tell you, then I would assume he was expecting you after work." He smiled and continued on with his paper work.

I smiled and nodded and headed towards his room. As I approached his room, I could hear that the TV was on and the volume was loud. I opened the door and he was propped up on pillows with a beanie on his head, three hospital gowns on, and a pile of blankets scattered all over the bed and chairs around the room.

"Hi my darling." I whispered as I walked through the door.

Riaan looked in my direction and smiled.

"How are you?" I walked over towards his bed.

He looked in my direction and put his thumb up without saying a word or making a noise.

Okay, he doesn't want to talk, that's fine.

I put my bag down in the farthest corner of the room and sat in the chair beside the bed. He had a horror movie from Netflix on. I don't like horror movies, so I was stuck between a rock and a hard place. I knew he didn't want to talk to me, but I couldn't stand to watch the gory, scary movie that was up on the TV at that moment.

After what seemed like forever, but I am pretty sure it was only a couple of minutes, I asked him, "Hey, so how was your day? How are you feeling today?" I smiled softly to show him I came in peace.

"How do you think Hadley? They pumped me with poison, I feel sick and I am completely frozen. I hate this God forsaken country" He spit out.

YEESH, I was not expecting that reaction.

"I am sorry my angel; tomorrow is a new day." I smiled as best as I could.

"Yeah, a new day to get pumped full of more fucking poison. Hooray to fucking poison pumping. I wonder what the 'side effect' is tomorrow." He said making air quotations and sassing his head back and forth.

"We take it one day at a time my darling. Be strong Riaan." I moved forward to put my hand on his foot under the covers.

"Hadley, just don't right now. If you want to be here, just be here. But be quiet. I am done for the day." He said staring at some Grim Reaper cutting up some poor, screaming girl in her matching bra and panties on the TV screen.

I really don't get the combination of violence and sex... girls running in lace panties and bras getting slashed up ... how is that entertaining?

I didn't end up staying long. Every time I moved a little in my chair, which was very uncomfortable by the way, Riaan would huff and puff. Needless to say, I took the hint and kindly excused myself.

"I hope you sleep okay tonight. Call me if you need anything, okay, my darling?" I said on my way out.

"I have nurses and doctors for that Hadley, that is why I am here. Have a good night. Bye" he said in a monotone voice staring at the TV screen. He didn't even take a second to look over in my direction.

What did I do wrong? For some reason, his behavior felt like everything was my fault. I felt guilty and ashamed, and I had no idea why.

The next day came around and I still hadn't heard from Riaan. It was breaking my heart that he didn't want me around. At the end of the work day, I pulled my buddy Dre into one of the offices in the dealership.

"Dre, he won't speak to me, what have I done? I am trying my best to be the best wife ever and he won't even text me back, let alone look at me when I am with him," I whined sucking back tears.

Dre looked at me with deep sympathy. "I am so sorry Had" He said and patted my shoulder. "I am sure he just needs his space and he doesn't want you to see him so sick you know. Maybe he wants to maintain what 'manliness' he has left."

I guess he had a point.

Riaan and I hadn't even had a chance to be a normal, married couple and go through a normal honeymoon phase yet. Shortly after he landed in Canada, it was blood thinner needles, popping tumors, blood tests, and scans. We went from a new marriage to me being a full time caregiver and him being my cancer patient, although, I never looked at it that way. He was still my husband. He was still beautiful in my eyes and I knew he loved me under all the anger. He was STILL MY HUSBAND and always would be my husband in my eyes. But Dre made a really good point, maybe he was looking at me like I was his caregiver, not his wife anymore. Maybe he had become so ashamed of who he had become over the last few months, that being a husband wasn't even on his mind anymore.

"Be patient with him Had. I am sure he will come around when he is ready, okay? Be strong!" he said chuckling and then smacked me hard on the shoulder.

"Thanks buddy, I appreciate your support." I wiped a tear off my cheek.

"Any time sista" he reached out for a fist bump.

My fist met his and then we pulled back and exploded that fist bump.

Hell ya! I'm still cool. I still got it.

I took Dre's advice and gave Riaan his space. I texted him first thing in the morning, wishing him luck that day and told him I would text him at the end of my day to see if he wanted me to come. It worked I guess, because when I texted him at the end of the day, he at least texted me back. It wasn't what I wanted, but at least he texted me right?

Ugh.... This sucks.

He didn't want to see me; we went a few days without seeing each other. He was polite in his texts and I tried hard to respect his space.

On his last day of chemo treatment, the hospital called me at 8:30 AM.

It was the first time I heard from the hospital, rather than Riaan. I rushed to find a quiet place at work to answer the call.

"Hello, this is Hadley." I answered the phone, trying to sound calm, but my voice squeaked at the end.

"Hi Ms. Olfert." A voice said on the other line.

Ms. Olfert? Oh Fuck, WHAT IS GOING ON??

"Hi, yes, this is she." My voice is cracking and I'm now chocking on my saliva.

"Hi, this is Lisa from GD6. I am calling to give you an update on Riaan." She explained calmly over the phone.

"Oh, okay. Is everything okay? Riaan hasn't texted me today. Do you need me to come in now?" I started to go OFF on this poor nurse, asking her all these questions.

She started to chuckle over the phone, "No, no Hadley, it's okay. We are great on this end. I just wanted to tell you that Riaan started to lose his hair last night. We find that it can sometimes be a very traumatic time for the patients. It seems to be for Riaan. He asked Chris to help him shave it off last night. He hasn't been too happy today. Were you planning on coming by after work today?" she asked.

"I was going to text him around 5:30 PM to see if he wanted me to stop by. Do you think he will want me to come by?" I asked, I was so nervous and knew I didn't want to hear the answer she was going to give me.

"Well, I suggest you text him as planned. But honestly, just with seeing him like this, I can bet he will not want any visitors today. I felt like I should give you a heads up." she sounded so kind over the phone. It was hard to stay positive with her though. She was telling me that she knew my husband wasn't going to want to see his wife today. It broke my heart.

I could feel the tears well up in my eyes as I was nodding silently over the phone. She could hear me suck back my tears. "Hadley, I know that this is hard on you. Probably as hard on you as it is on Riaan right now. Keep being strong for him, you are doing great. Stay positive my girl, stay positive." I kept silently nodding through the phone to her.

It was like she knew.... I bet she has done this a couple times before... THANK GOD!

Finally, I caught my breath, sucked back tears, and managed to spit out, "Thank you for taking the time to let me know. Thank you for looking after him so good for me. I wish there was something I could do."

"You are doing everything you possibly can for him. You must take care of yourself. We will take care of him so one day, he can take care of you again. Be strong my girl." Lisa said with so much positivity you could feel the smile through the phone.

5:30 PM rolled around and I sent him the scheduled text message. Almost instantaneously, I got a reply from him, 'Not today, thanks. Come tomorrow. Love you.'

Oh My God, He LOVES me. He really loves MEEE! Major self-confidence boost!

The next day was the day Riaan got his healthy stem cells injected into his body. Which means he only had two and a half more weeks on GD6. Once I got up to the ward and washed and covered myself up routinely with cap gown gloves and mask, I saw his nurses and waved a big wave and smiled a big smile. The desk of nurses chuckled and shook their heads.

I hoped and prayed that Riaan would be as happy to see me as I was to see him... but as I walk in all I smell is cream corn.

What the hell is that smell? Cream Corn? Who's got cream corn?
Wait, who, oh, that's my husband.

It had been a couple of days since I had seen him. He didn't even look like Riaan anymore. His face was skeletal and his eyes were sunken deep with dark rings around them. He reminded me of one of the Jewish prisoners from the Holocaust that I remembered from my studies in college. Well at least that was the first thing that came to my mind.

Where did my husband go? All I can think is that Cancer is like the Holocaust. I looked down as a tear slipped down my cheek. I had this over whelming feeling of deep despair for everyone who had suffered any kind of cancer in their lives. I need to compose my thoughts before looking up at Riaan.

Stupidly I say, "It smells like cream corn in here, any idea why?" as I sat at the foot of his bed.

"Yeah, the smell is me,' he whispered out as he sat staring at the TV searching through movies. "What do you want to watch?"

"Really? How come?" I couldn't get past the smell as I questioned him.

"It is the chemical that they freeze the stem cells with. Luckily, I can't smell it. I think it would make me puke." Still monotone and still flipping through the TV.

"Hmm, that is cool, I guess."
We silently watch some movie that I can't seem to remember. Riaan would smile at me occasionally, and all I could think was...

Thank God he still loves me. We are going to be just fine... or so I try to convince myself again. Boy was I ever wrong.

Two days later, I got a phone call from an Ontario number before 10:00AM. Now normally, I wouldn't pick up a phone call from an unfamiliar number, but with everything going on with Riaan, I wanted to make sure it wasn't in regards to him in some way.

"Good morning, this is Hadley." I said chirpy and cheerfully.

"Hi, my name is Joseph, I am looking for Hadley Olfert. Is that you?" this deep, authoritative voice asked over the phone.

"Yes, that is me. How can I help you today?" I asked as calmly as I could. My insides were flipping.

"I want to talk to you about Riaan Olfert, your husband." This voice grew scary and deeper with every word.

"Um, okay. Is everything okay?" I cracked.

"I am calling from Health Canada; Riaan was diagnosed with RSV this morning. His doctor has requested the release of antivirals which cost $35,000 a dose. Your husband's infection places all the other patients on the ward at risk, it is imperative that he begins taking these antivirals three times a day for the next three days. Are you okay with that happening?" he stated out candidly.

$35,000 a dose? What? Oh my God.

"I'm sorry, I don't understand. Should I be paying for these doses before he has them administered?" my voice was cracking, my eyes were watering, my stomach felt like a fist the size of Texas was ripping apart everything inside of me.

"No Ma'am. This call is part of the protocol for patients with your husband's medical status. Your provincial health care system will cover the costs for you. We do, however, need your consent as soon as possible because of the potential risk to all patients on the ward if we don't take immediate action." He explained like we were having an everyday conversation. "His virus could kill every patient on the ward, I am sure you understand the urgency of the matter."

"Oh, okay. Well, we must do whatever it takes to keep him alive right?" I asked chuckling nervously.

"Yes, something like that ma'am. You have yourself a good day. Bye." He hung up before I could respond.

$35,000 three times a day for three days, $315,000 worth of antibiotics pumped into my husband's body in 72 hours. That equates to $4,300 an hour... WOW, that doesn't even include the rest of his drugs, the cost of all the medical equipment, plus the staff looking after him. I have never appreciated my country more than I do at this very moment. Thank God my husband is now in Canada... In that moment, I felt so blessed to be a Canadian.

As soon as that call ended, I packed up my things from work and went straight to the hospital. As I was on the way out of the dealership, I texted my boss, 'Sorry, hospital emergency. Call you later. Thanks for understanding.'

Shortly after I pressed send, I got the response, 'Kick some ass girl! Good luck and keep me posted!"

I love my job. Best boss ever!

I rushed into the hospital and ran upstairs to the ward. As soon as I spotted Chris, I waved him down. He looked up from his papers and waved at me to give him a moment. I stood there impatiently and nervous, I didn't know what the hell RSV was and now he is receiving rounds of antivirals that I could never afford. After a couple of minutes, Chris came back to his desk and apologized for taking a long time.

"So, I got a weird call from the government today, Chris." I said perturbed and upset. I was so confused and stressed.

$35,000. Holy mother fucker.

"Oh yeah, because of the RSV. I always forget that they call the patient's caregiver. Don't worry it is a routine call. RSV isn't actually that bad, but because of the nature of the transplants and medical treatments on this ward, they need to be careful and give Riaan the Cadillac of drugs to make him better again. RSV is like a bad case of a head cold." He said nodding, like everything was okay, like no big deal.

"What about this $35,000 nonsense they told me about." I squeaked out embarrassed.

I was so afraid that the powers to be would change their minds and present me with a bill for the medication my husband needed to stay alive... Truth is, I am afraid all the time. I can't help wonder what horrible thing is hiding just around the next corner. It is like a dark fog that just won't lift, always lurking with dark fingers trying to pull you under.

"Don't worry about that. They have to legally tell you, but everything is fine. It is all taken care of. Have you spoken to Riaan yet today?" Chris said as he patted my shoulder trying to get me to calm down.

"No I haven't. As soon as the guy hung up with me, I ran over here. What should I do?" I asked, as tears welled up in my eyes.

"Hadley, everything is okay. Riaan is doing well. He isn't feeling all that great today. Like I said, imagine a really, really bad head cold." He said calmly, still patting my shoulder.

By this time, my breathing had sped up, I could no longer hold back my tears. This was all too much for me to handle and be strong.

"Does he need me today?" I said in between short shallow gasps for air.

"I think we can manage. Would you like me to tell him you stopped by?" He asked quietly.

I violently shook my head no. I didn't want him to know I was there nor did I want him to know about all the money these drugs were costing, even if we weren't paying for any of it.

"Okay, I will handle him today and you can text him that you will be coming by tomorrow. I will be off tomorrow, so it will be a perfect time for you to come by okay!" he looked at me concerned.

I nodded yes as I wiped my face and snot off into the sleeve of my jacket. I spun on my heels and left the ward. I couldn't bear to be there another moment. I felt terrible for leaving Riaan there without even saying hello. But the moment that guy called me, my heart started racing and I couldn't bring it back down to normal. I texted my mom and told her I was coming home and that I needed her to help calm me down.

I rolled into the driveway around 1:00 PM. I got out of the car, beeped my horn to lock my doors, and slowly made my way into the house. My mom was sitting quietly holding up a small glass of wine for me as she patted the couch to come sit beside her. She then pointed to a small joint that she had pulled out of Riaan's stash and had sitting on the side table. She held my hand and said, "There are times where words offer little comfort... I think this is one of them."

So this had become our 'shit hit the fan' routine.

Ah, a sense of relief for a moment. Sitting with my mommy. She'll make me feel better again.

Eventually my mom hugged me and said, "so $35,000 hey?"

I nodded, "We live in the best goddamn country in the world, I promise to never ever complain again at tax time". My mom chuckled, gave me a hug and said, "yes you will, we all will, but we will be very grateful having seen firsthand where our taxes are going.

CHAPTER ELEVEN

The Final Curtain

Riaan's RSV which actually stands for Respiratory System Virus, cleared up nicely after a week thanks to the designer antivirals he was given. That said, it did get worse before it got better. His mouth turned into one large blister and peeled off, so when he opened his mouth, it was black and looked like a raw, flaky sore. It looked incredibly painful, so I could only imagine how much it did, in fact, hurt Riaan. I watched my dearest Riaan dying right there in front of me, he was physically and emotionally disappearing in front of my eyes. When they tell you the patient will get worse before they get better, they don't give you the heads up that worse means knocking on deaths door for multiple days.

During this whole process of killing Riaan with chemo drugs in order to save his life, I watched my husband's blood counts deplete to almost nothing. They gave him bags of red blood cells to keep his organs from failing when necessary. Then, when his platelets had almost bottomed out, they wouldn't let him shave or brush his teeth for fear of not being able to stop the bleeding. The white board in the room showed Riaan's daily slow progression. From close to death to one day his blood counts miraculously started to go up on their own naturally. Just the way they said they would when Riaan's stem cells started to multiply and heal his body. My husband's body was finally starting to heal itself.

At this point, Riaan was eating very little and had no appetite. I was so worried and discussed my concerns with both of my parents. They, of course, said that his appetite would come back and that we could fatten him up when he finally comes home.

Funny how they have a way of making me feel grounded just when I need it most. I think we are going to be OK.

A couple of days later, I worked my ass off and sold two cars in one day, beating my personal record. I was proud of myself and couldn't wait to share this with Riaan. Closer to the end of the day, I got a call from my mom.

"Hey baby, I made something special for Riaan today. I am going to drop them off at the dealership, but keep it in the car okay?" my mom asked so excited she couldn't contain herself.

"Ummm, okay. That's fine. Why must they stay in my car?" I questioned.

"I did some research from the cancer websites and found some recipes for special brownies; I don't want anyone to accidently get into them while you're at work? They are packed with a ton of nutrition, anti-oxidants from dark cocoa, protein from black beans, extra vitamins from spinach, and a little bit of Riaan's happy stash... you feel me homie?" she said sounding so proud of her creation.

Mom was so happy with all her effort, I think she ate some herself, but she'll never admit that.

I took the brownies to the hospital right after work. I worked smart... I knew that Riaan would NEVER turn down pot brownies, so I lured him in early on in the day. I sent him a message.

'Hi my darling, mom dropped off special brownies for us tonight. How does a movie date sound?'

His response. 'Can't fucking wait.'

Whoo, I got a reaction... a positive one to boot!

5:59 PM rolled around and, again, I was out the door by six on the nose.

I hopped and skipped my way through the hospital with a Ziploc container holding a couple special brownies. I was so excited.

"It is nice to see you Hadley; he is doing better today. It took him some time, but I got him into the bath and bathed him today." Chris said with a gentle smile on his face.

"He didn't want to bathe?" I stopped in my tracks.

"It was hard for him, but once he got cleaned, he got happier. We washed away all the bad feelings. Or well, at least some of it." Chris said looking like this was all normal to him.

Having a good looking guy, who I presume to be gay, washing my twenty something year old husband.... That was not normal to me.

"Oh, okay, so are we good?" I asked cautiously.

"Yup, head on in there. I think he is looking forward to seeing you today." Chris said with a big smile on his face.

Oh hell yea he is happy to see me today! We are going to get stoned together and chill out.

I burst through the door with my arms in the air and a big, fat smile on my face to find a bald, skinny, yellow man sitting there

"Hi babe." He said nonchalantly.

"I have a little surprise for us!" I chirped.

Riaan calmly looked over at me and pushed out a smile.

"How are you not excited about this?" I giggled.

"Just throw me a brownie, let's get this party started." He said, in a monotone voice with no expression.

I decided to ignore it and keep being as happy as I could be.

"Want your yummy chocolate brownie?" I try being funny as I passed one to him.

He leaned over, winced in pain, and grabbed the brownie. In one inhale, he ate the entire thing and then chugged back a half a bottle of water.

He finally chose a movie and we got all settled in.

My momma did GOOD!

About an hour into the movie, Chris came in to take Riaan's vitals. As he was taking Riaan's blood pressure, he stopped and looked up at both of us. By that point, we had melted into our chairs, had a permanent grin, and were snuggled up happily.

"Your blood pressure is up a little Riaan, any idea why?" Chris asked looking right at me with a smug grin on his face.

Don't look at me like that, I want my husband to want to hang out with me. So I lured him with brownies...yes, please don't judge me. I was desperate to see my hubby happy and needed to feel any kind of positive emotion from him.

I smiled a big, cheesy smile.

"My hot, sexy wife is here Chris. How can my blood pressure not go up?" Riaan chuckled to himself.

"Plus, it hurts too fucking much to move and all I want to do is jump her bones, but thinking about a boner just kills me right now. Please understand bro, it sucks to be me right now." Riaan could barely contain himself, he was laughing so hard.

I silently chuckled. My stone was so intense, that I had lost my voice. So I sat in the corner and just silently giggled to myself.

We must have looked like idiots.

Chris shook his head, laughed, finished his paperwork, and left us alone.

The movie ended and we both melted so deep into our seats, it took us a minute to regain communication between each other.

"Hadley, babe, can you please grab me some water." Riaan asked me in a whispered voice, as he sat himself up to the edge of the bed.

I nodded, got up and walked around his room towards the sink which was by the door. I walked up around his bed and turned to face him. His yellow, gaunt cheeks turned to a putrid green color. Before I could react, he opened his mouth and projectile vomited chocolate goop that covered me all the way from my chest to my feet. I stood there in silence, not able to move or say anything. Riaan blinked a couple of times, scared to move in any direction. We both sat there like stoned idiots, covered in chocolate puke for a couple of seconds. Then we both started to laugh as I stated simply that all the nutrition in the brownies is now stuck to my chest.

I then walked over like nothing happened, filled up his water bottle, and left the room in the chocolate vomit covered hospital wear.

As I walked out of the room, Chris and Lisa both looked up from their desk and looked at me in question.

"Everything okay in there?" Lisa asked.

"Yup, I think we are fine. Riaan just puked this up all over me." I said displaying my new pukey outfit.

Chris put his head down, shaking it and laughing to himself.

I swear he knew.

"Is he okay?" Lisa asked.

"I think so, I just figured I would change and then go check on him. He looked pretty mortified staring at me covered in vomit."

Chris finally pitched in, "Let me go check on him quickly. I am sure he is fine." He grabbed a gown, mask and pulled rubber gloves over his perfectly groomed fingers.

Like I said, totally GAY!

A few seconds later, before I was done washing myself off and changing into new protective wear, Chris emerged from the room laughing hysterically.

"I am assuming all is okay?" I asked chuckling.

"Oh yeah, it happens. He will be okay. But you might want to hurry up and say your goodbyes, he is falling asleep already." He said pointing towards Riaan's room.

By the time I went through the whole bloody process of washing, changing, and protecting, I walked into the room to find that he was passed out, sitting up in his bed. He looked peaceful. I mean, he was yellow, skinny, boney, bald, and looked like he was dying, but he looked peaceful for that moment. I leaned in and through my mask, kissed the top of his head. He moaned a little bit and then started to snore.

It may have been a drug induced pass out, but at least he got some sleep.

I woke up the next morning feeling like a million dollars. I got to spend an eventful evening with my husband and I slept like a baby. Today was a new day and I was going to rock it and then go chill out with my husband again. It was going to be a great day.

By the time the Transplant team cleared Riaan to go home, he had spent 40 days in isolation. About 12 days longer than the norm, but those twelve days felt like an eternity. He lost a significant amount of weight and looked like a walking skeleton, a walking skeleton weighing in at a heavy 120 pounds. His normal color did eventually start to shine through again, which means he looked a little more like a human being versus a yellow tinged cancer patient, although the bald head and his skinny structure still gave it away.

"I'm going home, I'm going home, ya, ya, ya!" Riaan chanted as he packed his bags.

I sat on the bed watching him struggle to pack his things in his suitcase. He was happy to finally be getting out of the room he had been quarantined in for 40 days. He was a little bit stir crazy.

"Hey, my angel, can you please pack up the PlayStation, I need a break. I am tired." He asked softly, his spontaneous burst of energy dissipated as quickly as it came.

I nodded silently, got up and started to help him pack up the room. He sat down quietly, watching me intently, almost admiring the fact that I could easily pack up a room without becoming exhausted within a couple of breaths.

"Uggghhhhhhhh!" Riaan let out a huge sigh.

"What's up babe?" I stopped packing and looked up towards him.

"I am exhausted. I think I need to lie down. They told me this energy thing will take up to a year until I feel normal again. A YEAR Hadley, a bloody fucking YEAR!" he moaned out. As he finished speaking, he laid down into the fetal position on the bed, looking expressionlessly at the wall.

"Don't be sad my angel, you get to go home today! Isn't that something to be happy about?" I asked as excitedly as I could.

"Yes, but still. Humph!" He growled out, still facing that wall.

"Let me finish packing up, you rest and when I am done, we can get you changed and ready to go home. Sound like a good deal?" I giggled, trying to get something positive out of him.

He nodded yes.

I packed everything up and took it down to the car. When I got back to the room, Riaan was busy getting dressed into his street clothing again. His clothes hung on his twig like body. His tight polo shirt was now a baggy t-shirt and his jeans were too big to stay on him. As he figured that out, he grumbled, took them off, and put his hospital pants back on.

"I guess I am going to have to wear these out, since none of my other clothing fits me." he moaned out.

I didn't want to enable his whiney attitude or his negative outlook on things, so I sat silently and watched him until he was done. Finally, after a couple of minutes of him bitching and complaining about his clothing and his hospital pants, he was ready to leave.

Finally. I couldn't figure out why he wasn't happy to be alive and finally getting out of the hospital. It was the first day of the rest of our lives and I could hardly contain my happy.

I wanted to get him home ASAP. Maybe once he was home, he would be happier. We started to walk down the hallway and saw all the nurses were waving at him goodbye. I hugged everyone that worked with Riaan and thanked them face to face, they all handled him very well. I was lucky to have a little 'break' in taking care of him. By the time we reached the end of the hallway and were about to leave the ward, Riaan stopped cold. He put his hand on my shoulder and motioned that he needed a minute to catch his breath.

The whole lack of energy thing was real. We walked down half a hallway in a hospital ward and he was ready for an hour-long nap.

Chris saw that Riaan had stopped us and nonchalantly walked over with a wheelchair.

"Here ya go buddy, this should help make the trek to the car a lot easier. Take it easy bro!" As Chris offered the chair, Riaan fell into it.

They shook hands, fist bumped, and then we left.

When we got home, Riaan hopped out of the car, looked at everything in the back, and looked at me silently. We made eye contact for a split second, then he looked at the back of the car again, and then looked up at me. It was clear he was not wanting to carry anything into the house.

"I will empty the car once you are settled, let's get you inside." I walked over to the other side of the car and put my hand out for him to hold it.

He brushed my hand away and started to walk up towards the house, slowly and methodically. It was like he had to concentrate on moving one foot in front of the other.

We got into the house and my folks were waiting inside with kale shooters.

Yes, I have amazing folks. They would have NEVER done this if it weren't for Riaan being sick. There is a silver lining in everything... right?

"Hey there buddy, you look great!" my dad chirped out, thrusting his hand forward for a hand-shake.

My parents didn't come and see Riaan during his time at the hospital. He asked that no one else come and see him like that. We all knew how hard it was for him to even let me see him.

Riaan nodded in my dad's direction and held his hand out to shake his in return. My mom came into the front entrance, arms wide open and a big smile on her face.

"Oh my darling, I am so happy you are home. Welcome home, we love you and we are so proud of you." She said embracing Riaan with a hug. You could tell she was being as gentle as possible; her arms were wide around his body and barely touching him.

"Ha-ha, thanks Ma! I am happy to be back. I think I need a nap though. Is that okay?" He pulled back and looked at her with sad, apologetic eyes.

"Of course, but here, have this kale shooter first, get your greens in! Then when you wake up, you can have a brownie. I packed them full of beans and kale...BUT... they taste just like CHOCOLATE! Ha! Momma is goooood!" She expressed excitedly doing her little mom dance.

Riaan pushed out a smile and hugged her again.

He pulled back and looked up at the staircase, immediate defeat washed over his face. He looked down at his feet and then back up again at the stairs. He looked at it as if it were a daunting hike up Mount Everest, although in reality it was 13 steps. I grabbed his hand and took a step towards the first stair.

"You ready to go lie down?" I asked softly with a smile on my face.

He nodded yes, squeezed my hand, and we started up the stairs. We got to two stairs and then he pulled my hand back asking me to wait a minute. Step by step, we took all 13 stairs. It felt like the longest hike ever. Sometimes he was able to get in two, three, even four stairs before he needed a break. He sat down for the minutes in between each of the stairs. He rested his head on the wall, closed his eyes, and breathed deeply. Once we got him upstairs, he crashed face first into our bed. He took one deep inhale, pulled his face away to thank me for the lovely smelling sheets, and then he was out like a light.

I am not going to lie, it was so fast and so sudden. I stood there for a second staring at him, almost wanting more of a reaction. I don't think I completely understood the lack of energy he would have until that moment. It was seconds within lying down on the bed that he was out like a light and snoring. I poked him a couple of times, no movement, nothing... instant panic, but he was just sleeping. He was dead to the world at that moment.

All Riaan did after he got home was sleep, sleep, and sleep some more. I would get up and leave for work, he would be out cold. I would return from work and he would be sleeping still. I usually got an hour before I went to bed where we could talk and catch up. My parents tried to get him out of the room at least once a day to make it downstairs and to eat properly.

A couple of days after Riaan had come home; my mom had to go to L.A. for some business. She had been the secondary caregiver alongside me this entire process, so when she was packing to leave, the whole household was a little nervous to not have her around. She had prepped a bunch of food and made sure everything was in line prior to her leaving. The morning she left, I drove her to the airport before work. As we pulled up, she gave me a tight squeeze and told me she made a batch of special brownies she wanted me to surprise Riaan with when I got home that night. I pulled back from her embrace and gave her a cheesy grin. I was excited for the night to come so we could scarf the brownies down and enjoy happy high times.

A couple of hours into my work day, Riaan texted me a photo of my dad passed out in a hospital chair with his arms crossed at his chest, head leaned back, and mouth open. The text read; "I think Pa ate an entire row of brownies on the counter and I think they are Ma's special brownies...he is OUT! Ha"

I called Riaan to see what was up, as he picked up he was whispering; "Hey babe, all is good here, but your dad is knocked out. Ha-ha, he keeps rubbing his eyes, then passing out again, and we have only been here for an hour!"

"Oh my God, my mom told me about them, I guess she didn't realize my dad would get into them that quickly. Don't tell him, he will freak out." I whispered back. There was no reason why I needed to whisper, but I did anyways.

"I love you. I will see you tonight." He chuckled and hung up.

I got home after work that night to my dad on the phone with my mom. I walked in nonchalantly, headed straight for the kitchen to see the damage he did on the brownie pan. I could hear their conversation in the background.

"Gwen, I don't know how you do it. These hospital trips are exhausting; I am just drained mentally, physically. I am just downright tired and need to sleep. You are amazing, please come home soon." My dad exhaled.

Shortly after they hung up, I got a text from my mom that read, "Do you think we should tell him that he ate a brownie?"

I replied, "To be correct, an entire row of brownies from the 8 x 8 pan. I am surprised he is still standing."

Her response was to call my dad and encourage him to go to sleep, that he deserved it, and that she loved him very much. My dad hung up with her, hugged and kissed me and hugged Riaan, told us both that he loved us, and went to bed. That night, he slept for 16 hours and still wonders why.

It was nearing Christmas time and the snow had made everything white. I thought the snow made everything sparkle in the moonlight, but Riaan only saw cold isolation. Canada winters can be cold, but are definitely white. It's the perfect time to slow down and appreciate the ones you love. The closer to Christmas it got, the colder outside it got. Riaan's energy level was improving, but with that came impatience. I would come home from work and he would be up playing games on his computer or the PlayStation. When I tried to talk to him about my day, he would grumble and ask me to come back when dinner was ready. I complied and let him be.

My parents would encourage me to encourage him to try and get out of the room more than once a day.

"Honey, I worry about him. All he does is sit in his room. I am not even sure if he is sleeping anymore." My mom sat me down after work one day.

"Well, how can I get him out of his room? I know he is feeling uncomfortable sitting down here while you work. He feels in the way. When I try and explain that isn't the case, he just shuts me out. I am stuck between a rock and a hard place. How do I get him out of his room?" I sighed loudly and put my face in my hands. After all of this, now my biggest problem is to get my husband out of hibernation.

Each and every day, I would encourage him to leave the room and do something happy for himself. It was like pulling teeth to get him downstairs and moving around, but he complied most times.

"Come on darling. Let's go for a walk today." I delicately pulled at him to move off the bed.

"No, not today. I am tired!" He stated clearly, not letting me move him an inch.

"Why not today?" I said as I stood up tall and put my hands on my hips. I was trying to mock him and be funny.

"Because, this is my jail." He said looking forward, with zero emotion on his face.

"What does that mean?" I quickly realized my joke wasn't funny.

"It means that being here is as bad as the hospital. I can't sleep, I can't walk, I can't leave. I am stuck here, it is like I am in prison and it is freezing cold outside, so I am stuck in this hell hole." He looked straight ahead, without even hesitating on what he was saying. He was dead serious.

"Well, you know you can go downstairs and hang out with the folks and you know when I am home, we can go do things." I sat down in front of him looking into his expressionless eyes.

"No we can't, my immune system is still weak. I can't go out in public for another month, so I am stuck in this fucking room." Still emotionless.

It started to scare me that he was talking like this. I didn't understand why he didn't feel comfortable leaving the room. After that conversation, I left him in our room and went to talk to my parents about it.

"I just don't understand why he feels like he has to stay in his room. What can I do?" I whined as tears fell down my face. I felt hopeless, I wished that I could stay at home with him and keep him company. I wished I could change things to make him feel comfortable. But at that moment, I felt like nothing on earth would make him happy.

Christmas came and went. Riaan put on a brave face when the family came around, but when we were alone, he was down. His morale was low and he was starting to get frustrated and angry at the lack of energy he had. By New Year's Eve, he was able to go up and down a set of stairs in 10 minutes. That was an accomplishment for him.

I got the go ahead from Riaan's Doctors to take him out on New Year's Eve. I booked us a room at a hotel and arranged with the hotel staff for us to arrive at the back elevator so we could avoid being in too much public. I figured we could have a nice little get away and enjoy the evening together. That morning, my girlfriend Rachelle and her boyfriend at the time, Steve, asked if we wanted to meet for drinks before they headed out to their event. I asked Riaan and gave him the biggest puppy dog eyes I could muster. I really wanted to have a half normal evening and having a couple of drinks with Rachelle would give me that satisfaction.

Riaan agreed, "I think we deserve a night out. Actually, I think you deserve a night out my darling. You have been so good to me. I am so thankful that you are my rock." He leaned in and smooched me on the cheek. It sent shivers through my body.

"Oh thank you, thank you, thank you baby! It will be a perfect night." I squealed and kissed him back.

We packed our things and headed to the hotel as soon as check-in was available. I figured, since we spent over $250 for the night there, we might as well enjoy all the amenities as much as possible.

Riaan and I walked into the room. It had a king size bed, a huge hot tub, and a shower unit. It had a beautiful scenic view of downtown Winnipeg. I ran and jumped onto the king size bed and started to move my arms and legs like a snow angel.

"Look baby, I can roll around the bed without disturbing you tonight. Look, watch me roll around." I laughed and cried out loud. I had a moment of pure joy with such a big comfortable bed.

Yes, the small joys in my life make me really happy. A king size bed is one of them.

Riaan laughed and hopped on the bed beside me and started to roll around as well. Within seconds, both of us were giggling and playful and then one thing led to another and we were naked.

WHOO, yeahh!!

It had been so long since the last time we had sex. In fact, I couldn't even remember. It was long before his stem cell transplant and that started almost 60 days ago. After a couple minutes of intense foreplay, he hopped on and did his thing. I was too excited to even handle it. So luckily, I had my own happy ending, really quickly.

Pathetic I know. But please, every girl deserves an orgasm.

After what seemed like 5 seconds, which in fact was like 5 minutes, Riaan collapsed on my back huffing and puffing.

"Babe, I am sorry, I can't do this. I am too tired." He exhaled.

I manoeuvred my body to turn around and face him. I looked him in the eyes and said, "it's okay my angel. I am just happy you even got the energy to try. It was perfect."

"You came?" he asked surprised.

I nodded yes and giggled. "How can I help it? You are my husband and I love every piece of you. I was just SO excited about having that moment with you, I prematurely came... hahaha!" I shrugged.

"Oh, well that makes me happy! At least this skinny body of mine can still make you horny." He smiled and gently kissed me on the forehead.

I giggled and smooched his chin.

"Okay, if I am going to make dinner tonight, I need to have a nap. Why don't you go and enjoy that big hot tub and I am going to sleep until dinner.

I nodded and hit the tub.

We both had a couple of hours to rest and do our thing before supper. I wore a beautiful black sequined dress I borrowed from my mom, while Riaan wore a black suit he had. Mine, of course, was too tight and didn't fit me properly, and, Riaan was drowning in his suit. I am pretty sure all the weight he had lost, I had gained. It was crazy, my body was atrocious.

We walked downstairs hand in hand. There were plenty of people around us wearing beautiful, fancy New Year's Eve outfits and there was even a lovely jazz band playing live music in the background. We saw Steve and Rachelle sitting at a table in the corner. They waved as soon as they saw us. I was so grateful Rachelle remembered to get a table far from crowds.

"Yay, this is going to be a great evening my love." I said squeezing his hand and pulling it towards the table.

"Heyyyyyyy you two love birds!" Rachelle screamed as soon as we got close.

Both Rachelle and Steve stood up and the four of us exchanged hugs.

"Riaan, you look great! SO handsome!" Rachelle giggled admiring him.

"Thanks Rachelle. I tried to gain some weight, but you know, my body just likes to be skinny." Riaan snickered, while patting down his body.

We sat down and started to catch up. Rachelle hadn't seen Riaan since before his second round of chemo, which was roughly six months prior. Rachelle and Steve just bought a new house together, it was a big step for the both of them. I was happy they were so happy.

Riaan looked over at me and whispered in my ear, "I can't wait until we can do that!" I looked up and made eye contact with him and smiled.

In my heart, I was excited too. I just kept focused on living for the moment, who knows what is going to happen tomorrow.

It was about 10:00 PM when Rachelle and Steve had to go to their second function. Riaan and I hugged them goodbye and agreed to have one more cocktail before heading back to the room.

It was roughly 10:30 PM by the time we headed up to our room. Riaan had trouble picking up his feet and keeping his eyes open by that point. I had asked our waiter to put the dinner bill on the hotel room, just so I didn't have to worry about it. Riaan was my priority and he was falling asleep on me in the restaurant.

I opened the room with the key card from the hotel. Riaan instantly started to strip and make it towards the bed. I had strappy shoes on, so I sat down and started to fiddle to get the straps undone and take my shoes off. By the time I got the bloody things undone, I looked up at the bed and Riaan was passed out, curled up into the fetal position. I walked over and kissed him on his forehead, but he didn't even move. He was out like a light. That evening was, in fact, the most entertainment he had seen in months. He was active for about 3 hours total, which was an accomplishment in our eyes.

We slept until 10:30 AM the next morning. It was wonderful to wake up together in such a wonderful, comfortable bed, we both didn't want to move. Riaan made coffee in bed for me. We sat and snuggled until we reluctantly needed to pack our things and check out. It was a relaxing New Year's Eve and it was exactly what we needed and wanted at the moment.

"Next year, I promise we will party it up properly, okay babe?" Riaan squeezed me hard. I nodded while leaning into his body. I inhaled deep and relaxed within his arms. His scent and his body always gives me comfort.

It was the beginning of 2013 now, a new year, a new journey. I was excited for 2013 to start, 2012 was horrid. Even though Riaan was still exhausted for most of the time and would get really depressed every now and then, I believed we would pull through and that 2013 was going to be a lot better than 2012. I mean it couldn't get worse...right?

For Christmas, my parents bought me a year's worth of hot yoga passes. I was excited because I hadn't really taken care of myself in 2012, I had let myself go in more than one way. I looked at myself in the mirror and didn't recognize the woman I had become. My face was round, pale, blotchy, with breakouts all over. My clothing didn't fit properly, it either pulled in weird places or I just couldn't fit into anything anymore. I didn't like the unhealthy me I had become, so getting the hot yoga passes was a really awesome way to start my year.

I started to go every day. I would leave to work early in the morning, rush home after work and eat a quick bite with Riaan and my parents. After dinner, my mom and I would hop into her vehicle and head over to yoga class. At the beginning of the class, we would lie in a dark, hot room, resting and focusing on breathing in and out and letting the stress of the day wash away. I had to really concentrate to get Riaan, cancer, depression, and work out of my head. It was almost impossible to shut off those thoughts for the first few classes. The instructor would walk around the class and instruct us to breathe in and breathe out.

I breathe in.
I breathe out.

> *I wonder what Riaan is doing right now?*
> *Hadley!*
> *Breathe in. Breathe out.*

"Let the thoughts be there, just take note of what you are thinking. Then think about breathing in and breathing out." The instructor whispered to the class.

> *Okay, Cancer is on my brain.*
> *Breathe in.*
> *I just want my husband to be happy.*
> *Breathe out.*

The instructor could tell I was antsy and struggling with letting go of my stresses. She walked over to me and pressed down on my shoulders. She whispered, "Let it go."

I smiled with my eyes closed, trying my best to let it go. Yet these thoughts kept rushing to my brain.

She patted me on my shoulders again, "Don't worry, in time you will learn how to let it all go. Keep up the great work."

Within a couple of weeks, yoga had turned into my release. I craved to go, simply because after the hour in the hot room, I felt like I sweated out all the bad feelings and breathed in all the good feelings. I felt I was able to go home afterwards and be a better wife for Riaan.

I came home one night after class, super excited and happy. I had mastered a new pose in yoga class that day and I wanted to share it with Riaan.

"Babe, look at what I did today in class." I yelped as I got down on the floor and started to contort my body in a horrible attempt at 'Birds of Paradise'.

I am sorry to all the yogis out there, but that pose is just not flattering in any way. I am hunched over, my arms are twisted and contorted around my body and in between my legs. I try and stretch my toes as far as I can, but my leg still can't get straight. Either way, I could actually stand up, and keep my hands together, that was a proud moment.

Riaan sat there looking really unimpressed with my moves.

'What is the matter darling?" I asked as I untangled myself.

"Nothing, that is cool. Good job." He said monotone and gave me a thumbs up.

Hmm that is weird behavior. It surely wasn't because of my awesome yoga moves.

"Okay, well thanks. I am excited about it. Anyways, I am hopping into the shower and then going to hit the hay. I'm POOOPED out!" I giggled and leaned in to kiss him on his cheek.

He pulled away, looking down at the floor. He didn't say a word.

"Alright then." I said as I left the room.

I closed the bathroom door, turned the shower and the fan on, and stared at my disastrous face in the mirror. I have this overwhelmingly huge wave of anxiety for a moment. I stared myself down in the mirror, trying to mimic my yoga instructors voice in my head.

Breathe in.

Breathe out.

My breathing became shallow and quick, my eyes started to well up with tears, I started to sob silently.

Why? Why are you doing this woman? STOP IT!

I had zero control over my emotion. I sat there while the bathroom steamed up and sobbed uncontrollably for five minutes. Once I finally composed myself, I hopped in the shower and proceeded to ensure that I washed away all the bad feelings that I was feeling. I tried to focus on the fact that we made it this far. Riaan survived this much, only a few more months of recovery and we are in the clear. We had been through worse, we could see the light at the end of the tunnel. By the time I was dried off, I felt like a new person.

I wanted to share that experience with Riaan, in hopes that my new found positivity would rub off on him. I skipped down the hall towards the door whistling to my own tune.

I swung open the door and unwrapped my towel, like a flasher does. I laughed hard and as I focused in on the room, I realized I just flashed an empty room.

Hmm... That backfired. Where did he go?

"Riaan... darling?" I asked the empty room.

I heard him clear his throat from the spare room across the hall. I stepped backwards a couple of steps and peaked into the spare room. Riaan was lying down in there curled into a tight fetal position, staring at the wall.

"What are you doing in here Riaan?" I asked concerned.

He stared at the wall, without blinking, "I am going to stay in here tonight, okay?"

I stood there at a loss. I thought everything was okay or maybe it was just me that was okay. I didn't understand what was going through his head. After a minute of silence between us, I spun around and left him in the spare room. I got myself ready for bed and crawled into bed and focused on my breathing again.

Hadley, breathe in.

Hadley, now, breathe out.

I used to be able to tell myself "Chin Up Tits Out Girl" and it would actually make a difference.

...but it's not working right now.

Around 3:00 AM I woke up, I tossed and turned, and finally I hopped out of bed. Riaan was constantly on my mind. Him being in that spare room and not telling me why was bothering me. I wanted to understand how he was feeling so I could help him. I tiptoed as quietly as I could towards the room. The door wasn't even closed, so I peaked my head in and looked through the dark to check on Riaan.

"No Hadley, I am not sleeping." His voice stammered out in the darkness of the night.

"What's up my darling? Can't you sleep?" I whispered as I tiptoed to the side of his bed.

"No, I haven't slept in days. That is why I tried coming here tonight, to see if I could sleep alone." He wasn't moving his voice was so quiet I could barely hear him over my breathing.

"Do you want me to lie with you, my angel?" I whispered as I sat down next to his body?

He shook his head.

"I'm sorry love, it is dark, and I can feel you nod, but which way did you nod?" I asked trying to be funny and quiet at the same time.

'NO Hadley, I DON'T want you here right now. I want to be alone. I want to die. I don't like living like this." He whispered out.

"Riaan? What are you talking about?" I asked concerned, my voice started to crack and tears started to well up in my eyes. I tried really hard at holding them back and swallowing my cracking voice before I spoke again.

Riaan said nothing. I rubbed his shoulder and his arm a little bit, not knowing what to do or how to handle what was just said.

My husband just said he would rather die and that he'd rather not live like this anymore. Is that a suicide threat? Is this the type of thing that we need to be aware about and do something about? Is this an-

other fucking side effect that no one told me about? Is this the type of tragic story you hear on the news? Headlines reading "wife missed all the signs for suicide". God, what does this mean? How do I handle this? Do I trust him enough to leave him alone now? How do I leave him alone when he says stuff like that? All I really want to do is sleep. Maybe I can focus if I sleep.

I stayed with Riaan for about 15 minutes. I sat on the edge of the bed with my hand on his shoulder. I didn't say anything, but I didn't want him to be alone. He kept encouraging me to go back to bed, but I couldn't move. I was frozen with his words stuck in my mind. 'I'd rather not live like this anymore. I'd rather die.'

How the fuck am I supposed to react to that? If I overreact, I piss him off and if I underreact, I could be walking him to his suicide attempt. I miss the days when choosing between two pairs of shoes or a good bottle of wine was the toughest decision I had to make. Now, I'm choosing to leave my husband alone in a spare room or stay with him even when he doesn't want me there.

I woke up around 7:00 AM, I didn't sleep much that night. The words he spoke raced through my mind, my mind playing each and every possible scenario in my head. As I walked downstairs, my dad was making coffee.

"Good morning sunshine, I didn't realize you were going to be up so early on a Sunday." He chirped, as he grabbed another coffee cup.

"Yeah, rough night. I am really worried about Riaan. He said some things that made me feel uncomfortable." I stated, almost embarrassed to mention it, but I didn't know what else to do.

"Do you want to talk about it?" My dad asked as he walked over to me and hugged me.

As soon as he embraced me tight, I started to cry, "Dad, he said he'd rather die than live like this anymore. I can't believe my husband just said he would rather die. What do I do now?" I sobbed hard.

"Let it all out my darling, Daddy is here. Daddy hugs are the best. Let it out and we will chat about it." He continued to hug me until I could finally breathe again and calmed down.

After a couple of minutes, my dad offered a sleeve of his housecoat for me to wipe off my tears and boogers.

Like I said, best dad ever.

I wiped everything off, he looked at it, and said "Well that is gross."

We both laughed.

"I am going to bring coffee up to Mom, why don't you come with me and we can chat about it together, okay?" my dad motioned me to grab a cup of coffee and follow him upstairs.

We walked into my parents' bedroom, just down the hall from where Riaan was. On the way passed the room, I snuck in and took a peak. Riaan was finally sleeping; he was still in the same position that I left him in a couple of hours before.

"Good morning my two favorite people!" my mom smiled as we walked in.

"Good Morning!" my dad and I both said in unison.

"How are you doing this morning doll? You two sleep good?" she asked cheerfully.

My dad walked over to his side of the bed and sat down. He motioned for me to sit next to my mom.

"Actually we have to talk about something as a family this morning." My dad patted my mom on the knee.

"Okay? What is it?" she asked, the cheerfulness left her face as quickly as it came. She started to prop herself up in bed to pay attention.

I explained everything to her and held my composure really well. My dad nodded as if he was proud of me. My mom sat there listening intently, staring at me, looking into my soul, trying to get as much out of me as possible. She knew that she needed to listen to not only the words I was saying, but the tone of my voice, my body language, so everything combined gave her a true message at where my concern was coming from.

Once I was done, I let out a tear. "Mom, I just don't know what to do."

In her calm voice she always had a plan, "Okay, well, how about we call Doctor O. and see if you and I can meet her and talk to her?" she asked, hopeful.

I nodded. "I think that will be a good start. Can we call her now?"

My mom chuckled and motioned my dad to grab her phone on the dresser. "Of course we can."

She called and it went to voicemail. She left a quick voicemail for the doctor and hung up.

"How about we go to yoga at 9:00 AM and then we try her again? Go get your stuff, we will leave right away." My mom chirped and rolled over to get out of bed.

I nodded in agreement and got up and went to go get ready.

I collected my things and changed into my yoga clothing and just before I went downstairs to get into the car, I went and checked on Riaan one last time. He was still sleeping, thank goodness. I stood next to the bed and quietly counted to myself, figuring he was on hour three of sleep. "Well that is better than nothing." I whispered to myself.

"I am not sleeping Hadley. So three hours of sleep isn't right!" Riaan whispered.

He had startled me and I jumped a little.

"I am so sorry I woke you. I am going to yoga with mom right away. Let me know if you want me to pick you anything up on my way home." I leaned down and smooched his head.

"I'm fine." He grunted.

I left him, crossing my fingers, toes, arms, legs, limbs, everything I could cross in hopes that he would be safe and sound when I got home.

As my mom and I walked to the truck, my dad followed us.

"Don't worry my girls, I will take care of the house here. Riaan will be fine under my watch." He said as he leaned in and gave both my mom and I a daddy hug.

I love daddy hugs.

That yoga class was one of the hardest classes ever. I couldn't focus if my life depended on it, therefore I had zero balance. At one point, the sweat was dripping into my eyes and they started to burn. My foot was up above my knee resting on my thigh, standing tree pose. I wobbled back and forth, and back and forth. I tried to regain my balance, but not before my foot slipped and I stumbled to the ground. Everyone's eyes moved towards me, a puddle of hot mess on the floor. I got up, shook myself off and tried again. This time, I just stood there with two feet on the ground. I needed to be firmly planted on the ground at the moment. I was suddenly a tree with no roots; no way to keep my balance in the wind. I felt deep in my heart that a twister of a storm was just around the corner.

Literally and metaphorically.

After class, my mom and I got a hold of Doctor O. She agreed to come into her office later that Sunday morning to see us. After meeting her there, we all sat down so I could share with her everything and express my concern. I hoped that she would help me with a plan of action.

"Dr. O, he hasn't slept in days. He is depressed and last night he said he'd rather die than continue to live like this. I don't know what to do. I have been trying so hard to encourage him to stick with the re-hab plan he was given by the pain specialist. I count the Methadone pills he is still taking every day and it looks like he takes a couple of extra here and there. It is not like I can put my hands down his throat and make him puke them up." I whined.

Doctor O sat there for a couple of moments, thinking and deliberating. She then hopped up and left the room for a moment. She then returned with a sample box.

"This should help." She said pulling it out of the box.

She then threw the box out and popped it out of the casing. Both my mom and I looked at each other with a raised eyebrow.

"This is an anti-psychotic drug, but you are going to tell him that it is a heavy-duty sleeping pill. Understood?" She demanded and handed me the pill.

I looked at the pill and then I looked back up at her confused.

"You want me to drug my husband?" I quietly asked.

"Yes, I do. It will knock him out and when he is sleeping you get him back to the hospital and you get him checked into the psychiatric ward. I will call and let them know you will be there with him at some point within the next 24 hours. Do you think you can make that happen?" she looked at me over the rim of her glasses.

I nodded, "I don't know...I think so."

"Hadley, you have to. He has become a danger to himself and, in turn, you and your family. If he is speaking like this, we need to act. His reports from the hospital say that this isn't the first time suicide comments have been made. So once you are at the hospital, they will check him in and they will help him. But you must get him to the hospital. If you don't, we can call the police to take him there." She started to become very frank and demanding.

"I don't think the police are necessary, right Hadley? Riaan trusts you enough for him to take this pill." My mom patted my knee.

"I can't believe I have to trick my husband with an anti-psychotic drug and then check him into the mental ward of the hospital. Are we serious about this?" the tears started to stream down my face.

"Hadley, we don't take suicide lightly, this is going to get worse before it gets better. We need to act NOW! Okay?" Doctor O looked at me sternly.

I'm still waiting for these things to get better, it always seems to be getting worse, before anything ever gets better.

I nodded yes, put the pill in my change purse, and gathered my things to go home.

"Good luck and keep me posted Gwen. Hadley, you are doing great. Let me hug both of you." Doctor O swung her arms around mom and I.

Mom and I got settled in her truck. I sat there with it running and staring forward, befuddled at my next task.

"Had, babe, it is okay that you are doing this. Okay? You aren't doing anything wrong." As if she could read my thoughts. "Riaan needs you to be strong, his life depends upon it", my mom whispered in my direction, while patting my knee.

"Yeah, except for lying to my husband, tricking my husband, and then throwing my husband in the crazy bin. This is exactly what I want to do. Betray my husband! I started to sob again.

I cannot believe I have to trick and drug my husband, just for him to end up in a mental institute. There is no way this can end well. It feels like he hates me and this will surely be the final nail in that coffin. How will our marriage ever survive this?

We drove home and as I put the truck in park, I took a deep breath. My mom squeezed my hand and we both walked into the house. My dad was sitting on the couch with a cup of coffee in hand and his house coat still on. He gave us a thumbs up as we walked in, then pointed upstairs.

I ran up the stairs, "Hey Baby! How are you doing?" I made sure I said it loud enough so I could hopefully hear where he was.

I heard him call my name from our room. I opened the door and the room was spotless, the bed was made, all the laundry was put away. Everything was in line, except a backpack was full and in the corner behind the door, with a piece of paper sitting on top.

"How was yoga?" he asked while wiping off the top of our dresser.

"It was really good. I actually saw the doctor today too." I started, but then he cut me off.

"We gotta talk." Riaan stated and stared at me intently. I could feel his stare in the pit of my stomach. This was the storm that I feared.

In my head I screamed out, I PROMISE I AM NOT ABOUT TO DRUG YOU!!!! Please don't hate me. I am doing this because I love you. Remember, I will always love you.

"I need you to drive me to the airport right away." Riaan stated coldly.

"Wha- What do you mean?" I looked at him with pure and utter confusion.

"I am leaving." He stated bluntly.

"Where are you going?" I asked, thinking he was kidding.

"Back home. My flight takes off in five hours." Again he stated bluntly with no expression on his face.

"Are you serious, right now...Riaan? What do you mean you are leaving to go back home?" I cried out.

"Yes, I am leaving today Hadley. I hate it here. I don't like anything about this place, this place nearly killed me and I must leave right now." Zero emotion still on his face. He looked and sounded like a robot.

"What about me, what about our life together?" I cried out, still in shock about what he was saying.

The pill was still in the back of my mind. All I wanted to do was tackle him and shove it down his throat and make him pass out.

"You will be better off without me. So, are you going to drive me to the airport or shall I take a taxi?" He bleakly asked.

"What is going to happen when you get there? How did you get a ticket?" I asked, tears streaming down my face. I tried to keep it together, but I was slowly unraveling.

"My parents are picking me up. They booked it for me this morning. They told me that if I came home, everything would work out better." He looked straight forward, he wouldn't even look me in the eye.

"What the fuck Riaan! You can't just get up and leave our lives here. I am your wife; I have a say. I deserve a say." I sobbed out. I lost control.

"No Hadley, you don't have a say. You deserve a life without me." Riaan bluntly stated.

"Can't I be the judge of what my life is going to be like and who is in it?" I choked out.

"No Hadley, my mind is made up. I am leaving." He said straightforwardly.

"Are you coming back?" I sighed.

"No. I don't think so. All I know is that I need to leave, and leave now. So I am going." He stated, still staring at the wall.

"I think this is a mistake and you are having irrational thoughts. How about we postpone it for like a week, maybe then I can come with you and we can handle this together. Together Riaan, because we are married. That is what married couples do, they lean on each other and they work together. Don't run away like this. You will regret it." I begged him.

"Hadley, don't make me regret you. Take me to the airport." He looked at me and snapped.

Regret me?

"Regret me, what do you mean by that? Will you regret your choice about me, loving me? What do you mean Riaan?" At this point I was screaming at him. I was so mad, so confused, and torn apart.

My parents came rushing up the stairs and knocked at the door. Riaan rolled his eyes and motioned for me to get it.

My dad stomps through the door, "What is going on here, kids?"

I looked over at Riaan and then back at my parents. I couldn't even muster up the energy to answer them.

Riaan finally pitched in, "I asked Hadley to take me to the airport. I am leaving in a few hours to go back home."

My mom clawed her way through the door, "Going home as in South Africa, home?"

Riaan nodded, while looking both of them in the face.

He couldn't look me in the face, but he bleakly looked them in the eyes and told them that he was leaving. Why is he cowering away from me?

"Are you sure that this is the smartest and best idea Riaan? I feel like this is something we should talk about as a family." My dad pitched in with a serious authoritative tone.

Riaan nodded in agreement, "I am not part of your family, Sam. I am a liability to your family. In fact, I have destroyed a lot in your family. I can't be here anymore, this place is killing me and I need to get out before it does. Thank you for everything you and Gwen have done, I appreciate it. But if I stay, I die." He said looking right at them.

I felt like chopped liver.

"What about Hadley?" My dad said pointing at me. I was sitting there sobbing silently.

"She will be better off without me. C'mon we all know that. Hadley is destined for great things and I am not one of them. Well, I am assuming I am taking a taxi to the airport. I will call one now and wait for it downstairs. Thank you all." He grabbed his bag and excused himself.

My parents and I sat there dumbfounded on what just happened. I sat on the edge of my bed. The pill was still in my purse, which was still over my shoulder. I could smell my yoga sweat, I was nauseous. My parents both sat on either end of me and hugged me. I cried.

We sat there until we heard the cab call Riaan. I got up by myself and walked downstairs to meet him at the front door.

"I love you Hadley. Thank you for keeping me alive. You are going to do great things." He said looking at me with sorrow and pain in his eyes.

"I would be better if I had the man I loved next to me while doing those great things." I choked out.

"That is what you think now, but one day, you will look back and understand why I left. I am doing this because it is the best choice for you and your successful future. I don't want you to be a twenty something year old widow or a twenty something year old caregiver any longer. The doctors said to 'cut the cancers' out of our lives right?" He stated.

I nodded.

"I am your cancer and you must cut me out. Please understand. This is the only way." He leaned in and kissed me hard. The tears streamed down my face. Between the saltiness of my tears and the sweetness of his kiss, I was tangled with mixed emotion.

He pulled back, smiled at me as one tear fell down his cheek, he then grabbed his backpack and left.

I just sat and watched my husband walk out of my life.

He was gone.

ABOUT THE AUTHOR

Amongst her friends and family, Miranda Oh is known to be the storyteller of the group, always recapping crazy life stories and situations. When not playing the corporate part she can be found sipping wine and spending all her hard-earned money on shoes.

"When All Else Fails; Chin Up Tits Out" is the second novel in the "Chin Up Tits Out" Series by Miranda Oh.

I would love to connect with you:

www.ohmirandaoh.com

www.facebook.com/ohmirandaoh

www.twitter.com/ohmirandaoh

www.amazon.com/author/ohmirandaoh